A CLASH OF STARS

A Clash of Stars is the sequel to *A Meeting of Stars* and continues the turbulent story of Delia Summers. Heady from making the record-breaking flight across the Atlantic with Dean McArthur, she finds herself agreeing to marry McArthur, although secretly she believes herself in love with Paul Findlay, from whom she gained her love of flying.

But her marriage soon comes under great strain when it becomes known publically that it was Delia who did most of the work during the epic flight. To re-establish McArthur's reputation, Delia urges him to attempt another record-breaking flight on his own, but McArthur crashes on take-off. His feelings are further bruised when Delia makes world headlines by breaking the England-Cape Town record.

In a last attempt to save her marriage, Delia allows McArthur to compete with her in the famous England-Australia air race of 1936. The race and its outcome provide a fitting and satisfying climax to a story full of human passion and high adventure.

A CLASH
OF STARS

FREDERICK E. SMITH

ROBERT HALE · LONDON

To MOE SMITH
In affectionate appreciation of
your generous and valuable help.

Photoset in North Wales by
Derek Doyle & Associates, Mold, Clwyd.
Printed in Great Britain by
St Edmundsbury Press Ltd, Bury St Edmunds, Suffolk.
Bound by WBC Bookbinders Limited.

ONE

The first sight that greeted Delia as she opened her eyes was a white antiseptic ceiling. With her memory momentarily lost in the aftermath of shock, she shifted her head and saw she was lying in a private hospital ward. Alongside her bed, standing on a cabinet, was a telephone and a large vase of red roses. Sunlight, slanting through a window, was illuminating the roses like a theatrical spotlight.

A sudden and vivid return of memory made her jerk convulsively. Below her a river was glinting like steel in the moonlight. Beyond it were towering hills. Alongside her McArthur was giving a shout. "There's a field! Probably pasture land!"

No time to think. She had swung the control wheel and the dark field had leapt up at her. As she hauled back, she knew she had misjudged her height. There was a massive splintering crash and the aircraft, out of control, went slithering towards a huge tree. Another crash, a dizzy violent spinning, and then a tremendous jolt that had hurled the unbelted McArthur through the glass windshield.

Silence followed except for the sinister hissing of red-hot metal. Then pain as she had dragged her bruised body from the wreck and found McArthur, covered in blood, lying on the wet ground. Her cries for help had followed ... then the endless wait until lights had appeared and men had gathered around them.

Her relief at hearing that McArthur was not seriously injured had allowed exhaustion to take its toll. But one last urgent question had still to be asked. Where had they crashed?

The man's voice answering her had been full of admiration. "You're in Upstate New York, Miss. 'Bout eighty miles from

5

the city." Upstate New York ... Then she and McArthur had done it! They were the first fliers to make the perilous Atlantic crossing from east to west.

Fully conscious now, Delia glanced round for a bell-push. As she reached for it she discovered that both of her hands were bandaged. A few seconds later a middle-aged nurse appeared, clearly delighted at being in charge of such an illustrious patient. Her voice carried the flat New England accent. "Good morning, Miss Summers. How are you feeling today?"

Delia moved and stretched gingerly. The back of her head felt sore and her ribs twinged with pain as the nurse helped her to sit up. "I've a few aches and pains but I feel all right in myself. How's my co-pilot, Mr McArthur?"

"He's doing fine, Miss Summers. He should be up and about in a day or two. He sent you a note an hour ago."

Delia took the short note from her, written in unsteady handwriting. 'Hope you're O.K., honey. I'm doing fine at this end. Don't speak to any reporters until I've seen you. This is important. Love, Dean.'

Relieved, the girl lowered the note. "Then he wasn't badly hurt? He'd so much blood on him I thought his head was split open."

"No, the blood came from deep cuts and scratches. He needed thirty stitches but there was no fracture."

"Where is he now?"

"Here, in this hospital. In Ward Seven."

"Can I go and see him?"

"I'm afraid that's something only the doctor can decide. But I'll let him know you're awake."

Nodding, Delia turned to the huge bunch of red roses. "Who sent those? Mr McArthur?"

"Oh no, Miss. They're from the President."

"From whom?"

"The President of the United States. There's a card from him as well. Here it is."

Delia read the monogrammed card, then stared at the woman. "This isn't some kind of joke, is it?"

"No, of course it isn't. You're famous, Miss Summers. We've had a hundred reporters outside the hospital since before dawn this morning. We're having all kinds of trouble keeping them out. And there must be fifty cables for you already. Shall I bring them in?''

The girl nodded, then glanced back at the vase of roses. ''The President,'' she said. ''I just can't believe it.''

''I expect he was just as excited as the rest of us when the news came you'd gotten across.'' The woman's smile was a mixture of envy and admiration. ''My guess is he'll want to see you both when you're out of hospital.''

At that moment the bedside telephone rang. Answering it, the nurse glanced at Delia. ''It's the *New York Times*. Do you want to speak to them yet?''

Remembering McArthur's note, Delia hesitated, then took the receiver. ''Hello. Yes, I'm Delia Summers. What do you want?''

The room went quiet as she listened to the urgent voice at the other end of the line. The nurse watched her expression turn from surprise to incredulity. ''Are you serious? Yes, of course I am. But I'll have to speak to Mr McArthur first. I don't know. Today if they'll let me. Yes, all right. I'll phone you as soon as I've spoken to him.''

Left alone again by the smiling nurse, still light-headed from her injuries, Delia found herself wondering if Paul had heard the news yet. As always when she thought about Paul Findlay, her heart began to beat faster. The handsome young son of Sir Richard Findlay, a wealthy business tycoon, Paul had taken her up for her first flight when she had been only fifteen. She had found it the most exciting experience of her life and it had given her a passion for aircraft and a deep love for Paul who had shown her this new and thrilling world of flying.

From that day on, in spite of opposition from her family and friends, she had scraped and struggled to obtain professional pilot's qualifications. Although male prejudice had opposed her at every turn, one man, the chief engineer at her local airfield, had helped her to get her pilot's and engineering licences. Alan Wright, she knew, had fallen in love with her, but because he was a shy man and also twenty years her senior, he had never made the confession to her.

Not that it would have made any difference, she thought.

For her there had been only one man in her life, and although she had hardly seen Paul during those seven years of struggle, the kiss he had given her on the day she had flown solo had kept alive her dream that one day they would be man and wife.

The return of the nurse with a pile of telegrams and cables interrupted her thoughts again. Searching through them eagerly she passed over congratulatory cables from her family, from Alan Wright, and even one from the British Air Minister before she found the one she wanted most of all. It read: 'Well done, Smudge! A terrific performance. You've proved every one of us wrong. Love and admiration. Paul.'

She read the message at least half a dozen times before she turned to the pile of cables alongside her. When she had read them all, she placed them in a drawer of her bedside cabinet. The one from Paul, however, she slid beneath her pillow.

She was allowed to see McArthur that evening. At first his appearance shocked her. His beard had been shaved off and his head and left cheek were swathed in bandages. However the reception he gave her as she appeared in the doorway made it clear his injuries were only superficial. "Hiya, honey! We made it, didn't we? Come in and kiss a wounded airman."

The nurse in attendance, young and bright-eyed with hero worship, gave her an envious smile and left the ward. Crossing over to his bed, Delia bent down and kissed him on the lips. As he tried to catch hold of her to prolong the kiss, she laid a bandaged hand on his mouth and drew back. "You're supposed to be a sick man, remember?"

He grinned expansively. "I'm not that sick, honey." He indicated her bandaged hands. "What's the damage?"

"Nothing much. A few twinges and cuts and bruises on my head and hands. The harness saved me."

He reached out and turned her round. "Did they give you stitches on your head?"

"Yes. But only two or three."

"Just the same how come you've still got your hair and they've shaved me to look like a goddamned turkey?"

She laughed. "They've only shaved off your beard. Mine's camouflaged. They've shaved off two small patches of hair, so I got the hospital hairdresser to cover them over."

"So you've been to the hairdresser?" His eyes moved over the slim fitting, velvet dress she was wearing. "You didn't bring that dress with you either."

Talking to him seemed to bring home the full realization of their triumph after an unreal day. "You're not going to believe this – a couturier came to see me with a whole selection of dresses to choose from. And a shoe outfitter. Neither would let me pay a penny. And flowers have been pouring into my room all day."

His grin spread. "That's the way it's going to be from now on, baby. I got a cable from the President this morning. And they tell me he sent you roses."

"Yes. I still can't believe it."

"You believe it, baby. It's for real. You'll find that out when we go into New York tomorrow."

She gave a start. "Tomorrow?"

"Sure. We can't keep 'em waiting any longer: they're going crazy to see us. The Chamber of Commerce is giving us a reception tomorrow and we're to get a ticker tape reception later in the week. As big as the one Lindbergh got."

She sank weakly into a chair. Now it had happened it seemed too much to take in. Back in England her pilot's and engineering licences, won at great cost, had made little impact against male prejudice and it had not taken her long to realize that only by achieving some spectacular success was she likely to be accepted into the male world of professional pilots. Finally deciding a long-distance record flight could be the answer, she had sought for a sponsor.

Once again her sex had proved an obstacle. But Paul, now in America looking after his father's business interests, had put her in touch with Dean McArthur. McArthur, an American fifteen years older than Delia, had been both a playboy and a successful pioneer pilot but his star was now waning. In an effort to restore his fortunes he had decided to attempt the perilous east-west crossing of the Atlantic, a feat that because of the prevailing winds and the underpowered aircraft of the day had so far never been achieved. Learning from Paul that McArthur was in England and was expecting her visit, Delia had gone to see him in London.

McArthur, living up to his playboy image, had made a pass

at her at that first meeting. But although Delia was desperately keen to tap his pioneer flying experience and did not find his rugged masculine appearance unattractive, her love for Paul had precluded any thoughts of an affair with him. Her resistance however seemed only to stimulate McArthur's interest and he had invited her over to Ireland where the preparations for his Atlantic crossing were in progress.

Knowing she could learn from the visit, Delia had accepted his invitation, only for days of rain to postpone the flight trials. Gaining the impression the delays were affecting McArthur's nerves, Delia had offered to fly with him as a co-pilot.

He had brushed her offer aside but on the eve of his flight had tried again to sleep with her. When she refused him, he had taken to drink and injured his arm and back in a car accident.

Grasping her chance, Delia had made her offer again, promising that even if he had to rest most of the way, she would never claim more than an equal share of the flying. Knowing this was his last chance to rehabilitate himself, McArthur had been left little choice but to agree.

They had taken off the next day in a blaze of publicity. McArthur trying to cross the Atlantic from east to west had been news enough. A woman sharing the dangers with him was a sensation and the entire world seemed to have waited with held breath when their tiny plane had disappeared over the grey horizon.

As Delia had expected, the pain McArthur suffered had made it necessary for her to pilot the plane most of the way and she had been desperately tired before they sighted land forty hours later. Because their fuel ran out they did not reach New York which was their objective but that had mattered little. They had made the perilous crossing and their crash seemed to have made their achievement all the more dramatic and newsworthy.

Delia's sigh was heartfelt. "I can't believe it, Dean. I just can't."

He laughed, reached down, and picked up the top newspaper from a pile by his bedside. "Take a look at that. It's the latest *New York Times* edition."

The front page leapt at her. Three-inch banner headlines read AIR SWEETHEARTS SURVIVE CRASH. Beneath it was a photograph of the Bellanca flying over Nova Scotia. Taken with telescopic lens, it showed McArthur at the controls and her gazing out through the side window. Underneath was another caption. ENGLISH BEAUTY AND YANK ACE MAKE FIRST EAST-WEST CROSSING.

His laugh made her lay the newspaper aside. "You see what they call us, honey? Sweethearts. I like that."

She made a wry grimace. "You see what they call me? An English beauty. They've got a shock coming tomorrow, haven't they?"

"What are you talking about? They'll go crazy over you. What else did you get from those dress guys who visited you?"

"Just a coat, another dress and two pairs of shoes. I didn't feel I could take any more."

"Why not? This is the United States, honey. Those guys will make a million per cent profit when they tell the world they dress Delia Summers. You're a star now. The world's at your feet."

She realized he was right about the clothes. "When you've never had any money, all this takes some getting used to."

Since her arrival she had been feeling he was holding something back. His glance told her she was to hear it at last. "You've got money now, baby. Tomorrow I'm taking you on a shopping spree in New York."

She misunderstood. "I'm not going around trading on this flight, if that's what you mean."

He scowled. "Stop being so goddamned English! I've just told you: you're doing 'em a favour when they give you things. But that's not what I meant. I had a cable from the *Chicago Tribune* this morning. You remember – they're the ones who said they'd buy the story if I made the crossing." When she nodded, he went on: "Well, the deal's on. That's why I didn't want you to talk to any of the reporters. The *Tribune* want an exclusive on the flight and then my life story."

She laughed and kissed him again. "That's marvellous news, Dean. I'm delighted for you."

"Yeah. Ten thousand dollars. And that's just the beginning. We're on the gravy train again, baby."

At that moment she wanted nothing more than to share with him their good fortune. "I think you're right. I forgot to tell you I had an offer from the *New York Times* myself this morning. Only can we both do exclusive stories?"

"Sure we can. One from your angle and one from mine. After that we give 'em our life stories." Glancing at the door, McArthur lowered his voice. "But there is one thing, baby. We must keep our technical facts the same. We are keeping to the deal we made in Ballyvara, aren't we?"

"You mean about sharing the flying equally? Yes, of course we are."

"Good girl. Then we've no problems except maybe we ought to shop around a bit with your story. *The Times* doesn't always pay the highest rates and we might find someone who'll top them. What was their offer?"

Suddenly she felt hot and cold. In her embarrassment, she prevaricated. "It's quite a good offer, Dean. I don't think we could better it."

"Don't be too sure of that. How much?"

She hesitated again, then blurted it out. "Thirty thousand dollars."

For a moment the room went so quiet she could hear the rubber wheels of a trolley in the ward opposite. Then: "Are you sure you heard 'em right, honey? That's a hell of a big offer."

She nodded jerkily. "Yes, they repeated it twice. It is thirty thousand dollars."

TWO

For Delia the week that followed surpassed anything imagined even in her childhood dreams. The following morning, prior to leaving the hospital, she was visited by an editor from the *New York Times* who brought her an exclusive contract to sign. He also brought with him a tough-looking 'minder' whose purpose was to keep rival reporters at bay.

The *Chicago Tribune* were giving McArthur similar treatment although neither contract would be signed until a lawyer provided by the Bellanca Aircraft Company vetted the contracts. When they were found acceptable, both fliers signed them and then were led down to the hospital lobby where a dozen policemen were waiting to escort them to New York.

The police presence proved more than necessary. Apart from the hundreds of reporters who had been keeping vigil since they were admitted to hospital, people from the surrounding countryside had been pouring in since dawn on hearing they were being discharged that day. The moment the couple appeared in the hospital entrance a great cheer broke out and the crowd surged forward. Reporters fought to reach them, cameras flashed, and women screamed in both hysteria and fear as the crowd heaved and fought for a better view. It took all the strength and skill of the burly policemen to hustle the couple into the large waiting limousine. Half a minute later, with motor-cycle sirens screaming, the escort swept them off towards New York.

Their first stop was the Chamber of Commerce Headquarters where dignitaries from the New York business world were waiting to welcome them. In spite of the Prohibition Laws that were still in force, champagne corks popped, toasts were made, cameras flashed, and a hundred voices asked a thousand questions, some of which were parried by the accompanying pressmen anxious to protect their newly-bought rights.

When the initial introductions and toasts were over, the assembly began to polarize, the men to surround Delia and compete for her attention, the women to gather round McArthur. With Delia still suffering from the long flight and with her champagne glass refilled the moment she emptied it, she began to feel light-headed and it was a relief when McArthur broke free from his admirers and drew her aside. "Enjoying yourself, honey?"

She squeezed his arm. "I can't believe all this is happening."

Although his head and cheek were still bandaged and his arm back in a sling, his grin, lopsided though it was, left no doubt he was enjoying their triumph to the full. "This is just the beginning, baby. In a few minutes the mayor's going to talk to us about the parade he's giving us on Thursday. Next our newspapers are taking us out to lunch. They need our angles on the flight for today's deadline."

"What about our life stories?"

"They have to wait for those, honey. After lunch we're taking a break to do some shopping. O.K.?"

She had the feeling she was being carried along by forces totally beyond her control. "Yes, I suppose so. What happens after that?"

"Dinner and then we're going on Lester Morgan's chat show."

"Who's Lester Morgan?"

He grinned. "Only the most influential interviewer on radio. Politicians go on their knees to grab five minutes of his time. He's not only giving us an exclusive. CBS are cancelling their most popular comedy show so we get prime time too."

Her eyes were huge. "Does it mean we have to speak?"

He grinned again. "That is the idea of a chat show, honey. But it's no problem. He asks the questions: we answer 'em in our own words. Just be yourself and they'll love you."

"He will interview us together, won't he?"

"Yeah, I expect so. But either way it's no problem if we keep to the same story. Don't look so worried, baby. Radio's easy. There's only him and us and the mike."

"And a hundred million people out there," she said.

"So what? We wanted publicity, didn't we?" Conscious they were being watched by a score of guests waiting impatiently to capture their attention, McArthur lowered his voice. "You know something, honey? That crash was the best thing that happened to us. We made the crossing but nearly got killed doing it. That's drama, the stuff the press and radio thrive on."

She realized he was right. "Where are we staying tonight?"

"The Astor has given us a double suite for as long as we're in New York. The City's throwing a big dinner for us there after the parade. Everyone who's anyone in New York will be there. It's going out on the National network as well."

"You mean on the radio?" When he nodded: "Does that mean we'll have to speak there too?"

"Just a few words. Like saying how good it is to be in the States and what a wonderful city New York is. Lay on the cream, kid, and with your shape and looks you can't miss."

"They're not going to be much use to me on radio," she pointed out. "It's only my voice they're going to hear."

"So what's wrong with your voice? They love English accents over here. Just be yourself, kid, and you can't miss."

With an effort she pushed away her concern. "If we've got all this coming up, I want to go to a beauty parlour this afternoon."

"O.K. You've got time. The radio show doesn't start until eight."

She could not decide whether she felt frightened or euphoric. "It's too much all at one time, Dean. I keep thinking I'll wake up at any moment and find myself back at Brook Lane."

The flash of a camera caught his attention. Seeing him turn, three elegantly-dressed women, no longer able to restrain their impatience, ran forward and began showering him with questions.

She was not left alone for a second. As men of all ages jostled around her, striving to catch her attention, she caught a last glimpse of McArthur shouting back at her before he too vanished among the enthusiastic guests. "Take it easy, honey. Remember the sky's the limit!"

THREE

Lester Morgan's voice was as bland as his appearance. "I understand you come from Yorkshire in England, Delia. If I'm right, that makes you a Yorkshire lass, does it not? Or is it Yorkshire tyke?"

Delia thought her laugh sounded too nervous. "Lass, not tyke. Tyke means a man."

"Then Yorkshire lass it is. No one could mistake such a young and beautiful girl for a tyke." The bland voice ran on: "Am I right in thinking Yorkshire people think themselves a cut above other Englishmen? The way Texans do in the States."

"Yes. I suppose they do. But I don't think they really believe it."

Morgan's voice contained exactly the right blend of amusement and admiration. "I would suggest they do today. I would imagine they'll be dancing in the streets. Aren't I right?"

She shook her head. "No, I don't think so."

"In heaven's name, why not?"

"They're not that kind of people. They're not ..." She hesitated, searching frantically for the right word. In an instant Morgan came smoothly to her aid.

"They're not demonstrative people. Even so I can't believe they're not overjoyed today. You and Dean aren't just the first couple to make the dangerous east to west crossing; you're the first woman to do it. Have you thought what a boost that is for your sex?"

This was a reference she could not let pass without comment. "I hope it is. It was one of the things I hoped to do."

Morgan jumped on her remark like a stoat on a rabbit.

"Does that mean you're a feminist, Delia? A modern equivalent of your Mrs Pankhurst?"

In her nervousness she could not place Mrs Pankhurst and was grateful when he continued as if his question were unfinished. "Or like any of your other English suffragettes?"

"No, I've never thought myself one of them. But I hated it when they wouldn't let me become a pilot and an engineer."

"You felt it wasn't fair to be barred because of your sex?"

"That's right, I didn't. It isn't fair. Women should be given the same chances as men."

Morgan gave his inscrutable smile. "How did your family react when you told them your ambitions? Your father owns a garage in Yorkshire, doesn't he?"

"Yes, in Bridlington. That's on the east coast of Yorkshire. Dad didn't mind too much but my Mum and sister weren't so keen. My sister thought I was daft, always getting myself mucky with oil and grease."

She had no sooner finished the sentence when she felt herself turning hot with embarrassment. From her first meeting with Americans she had felt her accent must be noticeable to them and until now she had been careful in her choice of words. Yet now, just when millions of Americans were listening, she had used northern expressions that would surely make them laugh.

Her glance at McArthur, sitting in the third chair at the interview table, was a plea for help. Since Morgan had introduced them to his audience ten minutes ago, he had directed almost all his questions at her, a fact that made her feel uncomfortable. McArthur had shared the dangers of the flight with her: she felt he should receive equal attention.

To his credit McArthur had shown no resentment. Relaxed in his chair, he had been a picture of encouragement while Morgan had plied her with questions. The wink of reassurance he gave her now eased her embarrassment as she glanced back at Morgan.

If her words had amused the interviewer he gave no evidence of it. "So your mother and sister didn't like you doing a man's work? Did they try to stop you?"

"Oh, no. Not when they knew it was what I wanted."

"Just the same, it must have taken a lot of guts and

determination to work with men apprentices. Didn't they rib you a lot?"

"Didn't they what?"

"Didn't they pull your leg because you were a girl?"

"Oh, yes. At first. But they soon got used to me when I didn't act like a girl."

"You mean when you accepted their language and jokes?"

"Yes. I had to. I couldn't expect them to change for me."

Something in Morgan's glance told her he liked her. He turned to McArthur. "How about your views, Dean? Do you approve of women doing men's work?"

The big American grinned. "Not usually. I like 'em as they are. But this kid's different. She can break all the rules in the book as far as I'm concerned."

"Even to making an east-west Atlantic crossing?"

"That's right. How many men would have the guts to do that? She's really something."

"Let's talk a little more about the flight, Dean. Wasn't it a risk to carry a co-pilot instead of extra fuel?"

Relieved Morgan had shifted his attention to McArthur at last, Delia found her mind wandering. She wondered if her tiredness showed in her appearance. That afternoon, after shopping for two hours in New York's most expensive stores, she had found herself a beauty palour and stayed there almost until the salon closed, having her hair dressed, her nails manicured, and her face creamed and massaged. The very femininity of the parlour had seemed a necessary change from the masculine rigours of the flight and the terror of the crash, and she had emerged feeling a woman again in every sense of the word.

But her rejuvenation had been short-lived. The rigours of the flight, followed by euphoria and then celebration, were all taking their toll and she could feel her eyelids closing even as Morgan turned back to her. "How do you feel after such an exhausting flight, Delia? Very tired?"

"Yes," she confessed. "We didn't get much sleep on the way."

"I'm sure you didn't." He turned to McArthur again. "How's the arm, Dean?"

McArthur lifted and flexed it. "Not too bad. But the doc

says I'd better keep it in a sling for the rest of the week."

Morgan's nod was sympathetic. "I understand you had to take a heavy dose of pain-killers before the flight. And during it as well."

McArthur nodded. "Yeah, I had to dope myself. I couldn't lift my hand to the throttle otherwise."

"Didn't they tend to make you sleepy?"

"Yeah. That was the problem."

"Yet you still took your turn at the controls? You weren't tempted to let Delia do most of the flying?"

Realizing where the question might be leading and afraid the alcohol McArthur had taken that day might have blunted his awareness, Delia broke in quickly. "Dean didn't want to put too much of a strain on me. After all, I am only a beginner. Our deal was to share the flying and that's what we did."

Morgan pursed his lips. "I see. What you are really saying is that in spite of his pain, Dean cut down on his drugs so he could stay awake and do his share of flying. Is that right?"

She seized on his explanation even though she did not know where it was leading her. "Yes, I'm sure he did. I kept asking him to take more rest but he wouldn't."

"So it was just chance that you were flying when you ran out of fuel?"

"Yes. Dean had taken us over Nova Scotia and across to the mainland." For a moment her voice checked and Morgan eyed her curiously.

"And then?"

She recovered. "Then I took over for the last stretch. It just worked out that way."

Across the table McArthur was thanking her with his eyes. Morgan turned to him. "In hindsight, Dean, I suppose you wish now you'd stayed at the controls on the last lap?"

McArthur frowned. "Yeah, I suppose so. But when you've been flying as long as we had, you don't think that clearly." As Delia relaxed, McArthur paid back some of his debt to her. "Anyway, it would have made no difference. She handled that crash landing like a professional. I couldn't have done it better."

If Morgan's questions had been a probe, he gave no sign of it as he smiled at Delia. "What does our Yorkshire lass think of that? I imagine you couldn't wish for a higher tribute. What are your plans for the future? I understand your plane is a total write-off."

Delia nodded. "Yes. I believe souvenir hunters have stripped it clean. We haven't any plans at the moment. I think we're still recovering."

"That's understandable enough. But do you intend staying in the States for a while?"

Her voice was eager. "I'd like to. Everyone has been so kind."

"That's because we admire you, Delia. You'll see how much we admire you on Thursday. Are you looking forward to the parade?"

Knowing the crisis was over, she found herself relaxing. "Yes. Very much. Only I'm nervous."

"You're nervous! You fly across the Atlantic but feel nervous at meeting your fans. Delia, I think that's beautiful."

She smiled at him. "It's different, isn't it?"

"I'll say it's different. On Thursday you'll find out what New York thinks about a Yorkshire lass who has the courage to take on the Atlantic and an American flier who, although injured, helped her to make aviation history. Ladies and gentlemen, I give you Delia Summers and Dean McArthur."

Fifteen minutes later she and McArthur were climbing into a huge CBS limousine. As they settled into its soft leather seats and the chauffeur closed the door, McArthur squeezed her arm. "You're tops, baby. Thanks."

She turned to him. "I couldn't decide whether he was probing or not. What did you think?"

"I don't know either. You can't get behind that goddamned mask of his. But it's O.K. You handled it well."

She was not so sure. "The trouble is, he said enough to start other people wondering. We'll both have to be very careful what we say."

"No, you said all the right things, baby. Everything's going to be fine from now on."

Although at her request he had not had a drink since lunchtime, he had drunk enough beforehand for her to question his judgement. But before she could say more, he pulled her towards him. "What about a little kiss now for your co-pilot, baby?"

After all that had happened she felt unable to deny him that. Nor did she find it unpleasant to be in his arms in the erotic ambience of the limousine. It was only when his hands began to wander that she straightened and pushed him away. "Give you an inch and you take a mile. Anyway, we're both too tired. Let me look out of the window. Remember I haven't seen New York at night."

Fascinated, she watched the countless neon lights drift past while McArthur pointed out landmarks to her. Cosy in the limousine, unmolested for the first time that day, she was almost sorry when they drew up outside the hotel.

Nevertheless the circus of hospitality commenced again the moment they entered the foyer and found the manager waiting to welcome them. Delia was given a posy and then they were taken upstairs to a lavish pent-house suite. As the manager opened the door and waved them inside, Delia gave a gasp of surprise. The lounge they entered was filled with flowers. Huge blooms stood in vases on the tables, the window ledges, even in baskets on the walls, their scent filling the air like heady perfume. Spinning round, Delia clapped her hands together. "Dean, look at all these flowers! Aren't they just beautiful?"

The manager, middle-aged, blasé, used to the spoilt appetites of wealthy guests, smiled at her uninhibited delight. "It is our pleasure, Miss Summers. I'm happy that you like them. When you're both ready, ring the switchboard and my assistant will take you down to the Blue Room."

The Blue Room proved to be a magnificent dining-room where a lavish buffet supper and two dozen of the hotel's most distinguished guests were awaiting them. Although liquor was not openly on display, Delia soon discovered the cider she was given tasted remarkably like champagne while McArthur, after a few words to the manager, was clearly content with the amber liquid he was offered. With the waiters attentive and with toast following toast, he was soon able to compensate for his abstinence that afternoon and when the celebrations were finally over, she had to assist him upstairs to their suite.

Light-headed herself from the champagne she had drunk, the scent of the flowers seemed almost overpowering as she steered him across the room to an armchair. "Sit there," she panted. "And I'll have some coffee sent up."

He grimaced comically at her as he sank down. "I don't want coffee. I want you, baby. All to myself."

"That was whisky you were drinking tonight, wasn't it?" she said. "I was hoping you wouldn't be able to get it over here."

He grinned. "If you've got the money or you're well known, you can get all the hooch you want. Didn't you know that?"

"I know that the doctors said you weren't supposed to drink spirits for a few days. And you look as if you've drunk enough to float a battleship."

"C'mon, honey. It's a special day."

"It's a special day for the rest of the week. And I'm wondering how you're going to cope with it."

"Quit treating me as if you were my old mother, baby. Come and sit on my knee. I've lots of things to tell you."

"I'll bet you have. Then you don't want coffee?"

"No. I've told you what I want. You, baby. You, you, you."

She was thinking about their radio interview and the thought that had come to her when she was telling Morgan that McArthur had flown them over Nova Scotia. If she questioned him about it now, there was a greater chance of learning the truth than when he was sober. Yet was it important enough for her to bring it up at all?

She decided it was not. Dean was what he was, and when all was said and done, she owed him everything that she had become. Reaching down, she put an arm beneath his shoulder. "You're too drunk to know what you're saying. Come on. Let's get you to bed."

He allowed her to help him into the bedroom. As they reached the bed, he tried to put his good arm around her. Pulling away, she gave him a push. With his knees catching the edge of the bed he toppled backwards with a grunt of alarm. Swinging up his legs so that he was lying supine, she pulled off his shoes and then drew back. "There. Now go to sleep. We've got a hard day tomorrow."

He lifted his head a few inches from the pillow and reached out his hand. "You're not really going, are you, honey? Not tonight."

She did not know whether it was a trick of the light or the effect of his bandages but for a moment she had a vision of a lonely man disguising his loneliness with sex, self-assertion and danger. The vision disappeared almost immediately as he tried to catch her arm but not the memory of the debt she owed him. It made her wonder what her response would have been if she had not received the cable from Paul. She had drunk enough that day to lower her own sexual threshold and there was no denying that their shared ordeal had brought them closer together. To soften her refusal, she appealed to his sense of humour, an attribute she particularly liked. "Dean, take a look at yourself. If we went to bed together tonight, it would be a disaster."

He was not too drunk to grin back. "Don't talk like that, baby. Maybe I could rise to the occasion. What's the harm in trying?"

"You're drunk, Dean. Take my word for it. Get your head down and go to sleep."

She was halfway to the door when his slurred voice checked her. "I know what it is with you, baby."

"What?" she smiled.

"You're an old-fashioned girl, that's what you are. You've got to be married before you can do it. Isn't that right?"

"Do you think so, Dean?"

"Yeah, that's it. Look, baby, that's O.K. by me. I've never liked being hitched but you're different. What do you say?"

In spite of his condition, she found his offer moved her. "That's not why I'm holding off, Dean. I wouldn't do a thing like that to you."

He did not hear her. "They're callin' us 'Sweethearts of the Air', aren't they? Then let's show 'em they're right. Let's get hitched. What d'you say, honey? We can fly to Reno and ..."

His voice faded away. Tip-toeing back to the bed she found he was fast asleep. Smiling, she pulled a blanket over him. She gazed down at his bandaged face for a moment, then on an impulse she bent down and kissed him. A moment later she switched off the light, closed his door, and crossed over to her own room.

FOUR

The scraps of paper thrown from the towering skyscrapers were as numerous as snowflakes as they came fluttering down. Ticker tapes, unrolling as they fell, draped over the excited crowds that packed the sidewalks. Cheers reverberated deafeningly across the concrete canyons. Bands played triumphant music; police cars and motor cycles added to the din with their sirens. The entire city of New York appeared to have turned out and to be taking part in the rapturous welcome.

Delia and McArthur were perched on the tonneau of a huge convertible. As a strip of ticker tape fell on the American's head and he brushed it away, she leaned towards him. "How are you feeling now?"

His grimace turned into a grin as he remembered where he was. "Terrible, honey. Like a dog's dinner."

She smiled gaily at a large bosomed woman who threw a bunch of flowers into the car. "Serve you right," she said. "The biggest day of your life and you have to spoil it with a hangover."

The previous day had been another mad whirl of parties and functions and in the evening they had been taken to the 21 Club, New York's most famous speakeasy. There McArthur had been joined by three buddies from his old barnstorming days and the result had been a wild drinking session that had only ended when Delia and her two police bodyguards had half-carried him to a taxi at three in the morning.

Delia herself was feeling more confident than at any time since their dramatic arrival. For this she owed much to the hotel's beautician who, after putting the final touches to her hair and face, had helped her choose what to wear. The choice

24

had been a blue, slim-fitting costume that not only showed off her shapely figure but acted as a foil for her blonde hair (on the woman's advice she was not wearing a hat). With the beautician's assurance that she looked a picture of fashion and elegance, with the autumn day sunny, and the crowds overflowing with goodwill and admiration, she was at last enjoying her success to the full.

McArthur on the other hand had complained of a severe hangover since being awakened at six a.m. Nevertheless he was putting on a brave front, waving to the cheering crowds and blowing kisses at his female admirers who oo'd and aah'd in sympathy at his bruised and plastered face.

A snowstorm of paper came tumbling down when they entered the heart of Manhattan. It covered the bonnet and piled up on the leather seats of the convertible. Overhead an aircraft was dragging a banner behind it. As it flew along one of the man-made canyons, Delia read its message. NEW YORK WELCOMES AVIATION SWEETHEARTS.

McArthur followed her eyes. Wincing at the bright sunlight, he turned to her. Unable to hear him for the din, she leaned closer. He put his mouth to her ear. "See that, honey? They've all got the same idea. What about it?"

She was surprised that he remembered. "Why do you want to spoil things? Don't you know married couples haven't any glamour?"

"Who says so?"

"All the women's magazines. You'll lose all your female fans if you get married. Anyway, you've had two goes at it. Why put your head in the noose a third time?"

He grinned. "Third time's lucky, baby. Haven't you heard?"

The sidewalks and roads were packed even more tightly as they neared the City Hall. With music blaring a welcome, with people cheering and waving both their national flags, it was a scene of colour, movement, and intense excitement.

The resplendent figure of the mayor could now be seen walking down the steps to meet them. Suddenly, without any warning, McArthur caught hold of her and gave her a passionate kiss.

A cheer burst out that seemed to rock the massive buildings.

A flock of pigeons, perched high on the roof of the City Hall, took flight and exploded like confetti into the sky. The crowd pressed closer, the flags waved more joyously, while cameras clicked on all sides.

Furious with him, Delia was about to pull away when she realized that any sign of dissent would become headline news all over the world. Instead, unseen by the cheering onlookers, she stabbed the heel of her shoe on his foot and ground it down painfully. "You bastard," she muttered as he released her. "That's playing it dirty."

To her surprise he looked both embarrassed and contrite as he sat back. "Sorry, honey. I guess I was just carried away by all this excitement."

She was still trying to decide whether it was an impulsive gesture or not when the convertible pulled up at the foot of the City Hall steps.

If proof were needed of how quickly Americans can move, it was evident in the Astor that same night. Crystal chandeliers shone down brilliantly on over a thousand elegantly-dressed men and women, all contacted by the City Administration in the last three days. They were entertained by two famous dance bands, both of whom were giving their services free in honour of the two fliers. Union Jacks as well as the Stars and Stripes hung from every wall. In a side room a buffet supper was laid out among vases of flowers. Only soft drinks were on display but a guest had only to whisper in the ear of a waiter and one coloured drink was quickly exchanged for another. By this time Prohibition was a farce in New York.

Delia and McArthur had been introduced to the guests at eight-thirty. From then on the girl had been inundated by men eager to talk and dance with her. For a while her youth and the excitement of being a celebrity had enabled her to dance with every man who had won a way to her side. But as the hours passed and she was handled like some exotic package from one man to another, names began to escape her and faces started to look alike. By eleven p.m. the effect of the last few exhausting days had caught up with her and she tried to escape into one of the ante-rooms.

But there was no escape. Men pursued her, clustered round

her, offered to fetch her food and drink. She longed for McArthur to arrive and rescue her but she had not seen him for over an hour. Just as she was about to make the Ladies Room an excuse for privacy, an English voice made her start and turn. She felt the blood drain from her cheeks when she saw Paul pushing through the cordon of admirers to reach her.

Like the other men he was wearing evening clothes but to her he stood out like a prince among beggars. Tears blurred her eyes as he caught hold of her hands, drew her forward, and kissed her cheek. "Hello, Delia. My warmest congratulations."

For a moment she was terrified that she was going to break down. "Paul! How lovely to see you again. I didn't know you were in New York."

"I only arrived this evening. I couldn't get here any sooner." His eyes moved over her admiringly. "You look wonderful."

Although emotion was threatening to overwhelm her, all her physical weariness fell away. "So do you! Just as I've always remembered you." Conscious of the envious eyes watching them, she glanced round. "Can't we go somewhere quieter to talk?"

Disappointed men fell back as he laid a hand on her bare arm and led her to a far corner of the room. The skin where he touched her took on a sensitivity of its own and her legs felt weak. "Thanks so much for the cable, Paul. It meant a great deal to me."

"I couldn't believe it when I heard McArthur was letting you fly with him. I'd never heard of anything more irresponsible."

Her eyes were moving over his dark hair and good-looking face. He was still the handsomest man she'd ever met, she thought. "It wasn't his fault. I asked to fly with him."

"That's not the point. He should never have let you."

The knowledge he cared about her was like champagne, filling her bloodstream with bubbles of happiness. "I'm glad he did. I'd never have got to America and seen you again if he hadn't, would I?"

A shadow crossed his eyes. It vanished when he gave the

laugh she remembered so well. "It's all like a fairy story, Smudge. I remember you as a little girl with a grubby face. Now here you are, the toast of New York and the world. It's unbelievable."

She wished her eyes would stop blurring. "I owe it all to you, Paul. If you hadn't taken me up that day, nothing like this would have happened. I'd probably still be working in my Dad's garage."

"Instead you've got the world at your feet. What are you planning to do next?"

"I haven't any plans. Only that I'd like to stay in America for a while." She knew her question was ingenuous but with him she could never be anything but herself. "Where are you living at the moment?"

"Still at the same address. I'm based in Philadelphia although I have to travel a good deal. I was down south when you came crashing in."

She was feeling almost euphoric being with him again. "Crashing in sums it up perfectly. It wasn't the glamorous ending we hoped for."

They laughed together, then his voice turned serious. "Thank heaven it turned out no worse. It was an enormous relief when I heard you weren't badly hurt."

"Was it, Paul?" she asked.

"Of course it was." As he paused, she wondered why she felt he was waiting for an answer to a question he was reluctant to ask. "How are things in general, Smudge?"

The wording of his question puzzled her. "They're wonderful. I've never been so happy in my life."

A weight seemed to lift from him, puzzling her further. "You haven't? That's wonderful. I'm so glad."

She laughed. "It's hardly surprising, is it? I've achieved the thing I dreamed about and now I've met you in New York. What more could a girl want?"

Suddenly concern seemed to mingle with his relief. "Did you get my last letter?"

"Which one?" she asked.

"The one I wrote from Philadelphia. Just over three weeks ago."

"No. My Mum and Dad would forward it on but our

airstrip was right out in the blue, so I suppose it was delayed. But we left instructions before take-off for our mail to be sent on. It might be on the mail boat that docked today." Her eyes shone at him. "I hope so. I love getting your letters, Paul." Then she noticed his expression. "What's the matter?"

He hesitated. Then, as he was about to answer, she saw McArthur appear in the doorway. Whereas before she had wanted his company, now she felt intense disappointment that he was about to interrupt her unexpected tête-à-tête with Paul.

The big American glanced round, then caught sight of her. As he started down the room, his appearance drew the attention of whispering guests. Drained by the traumas and the celebrations of the week but supported by the alcohol he had drunk, it looked now as if the evening had put the final seal on his exhaustion. His walk was unsteady and his heavy-lidded eyes were half-closed.

Putting on the best face she could, Delia made the introductions. "Dean, meet Paul Findlay. We're old friends. You've heard me talk about him."

"Yeah. Often." There was no friendliness in the American as he shook hands briefly with Paul. "You're the guy who asked Sorenson to get in touch with me, aren't you? About meeting Delia in London?"

"That's right. Congratulations on your flight. It was a terrific achievement. How's your arm coming along?"

"It's O.K. The doc says I can let it loose in a couple of days."

"That's good news. What are you planning to do next?"

McArthur glanced at Delia. "We haven't any plans right now. I guess a rest would do us both good."

Anxious to talk to Paul alone, Delia snatched at the opportunity his words offered without thinking. "You're looking as if you could pass out at any time. Why don't you make your excuses and go up to the suite? Everyone will understand."

It was a bad mistake. The big American's face darkened. "What is it, baby? You trying to get rid of me all of a sudden?"

Recognizing the danger signs, Paul broke in quickly. "That reminds me: I must get back myself. I've some papers to read before tomorrow.''

She could have cried with disappointment. "But we've so much to talk about. Can't we meet tomorrow? Where are you staying?''

He hesitated. "The Plaza.''

"Then can't I give you a call in the morning? What time will you be going out?''

"Not before ten-thirty.''

"Then I'll phone you at ten. Is that all right?''

"Yes, I'll be there.'' Paul turned to the sullen McArthur. "Perhaps we could all have lunch together. I shan't be leaving town until the late afternoon. I'd like to entertain you and celebrate your engagement.''

Delia gave a gasp. McArthur stared at him. "What engagement?''

It was the Englishman's turn to look surprised. "Your engagement to Delia.'' Then, noticing their expressions: "Isn't it true? The late evening edition of *The Times* says it's only a matter of days. It's on all the billboards too.''

Delia glanced at McArthur before turning back to Paul. "Is there a photograph of us in the paper? In the car, outside the City Hall?''

He smiled. "Yes. I suppose that's why I found the report so convincing.''

Her condemning eyes moved on McArthur again. "You and a few million others,'' she said bitterly. "Well, it's not true. We've no intention of getting engaged, now or later. We're just partners. Nothing more. Isn't that true, Dean?''

Guilt and jealousy brought back the American's aggression. "I don't know what the hell we are, baby. I'm getting out of here. You two stay and go on talking about the old days.''

Paul checked him. "No, please. I only intended to stay a few minutes. I must go now.'' He smiled at Delia. "Give me a ring in the morning and let's all try to meet for lunch.''

Nodding at McArthur, he turned away. Delia watched his slim figure, with its slight distinguished limp, leave the room. Tears of distress and anger were running down her cheeks as she turned back to McArthur. "I'm going upstairs now. No, don't try to come with me or I won't go. I don't want to hear you or see you again tonight.''

FIVE

It was after two o'clock that morning when her bedroom door burst open. Startled she sat up and saw McArthur's silhouette framed in the doorway. "What do you want?"

Without speaking he walked unsteadily to a chair and sank into it. Switching on a bedside lamp, she saw his hair was dishevelled and the plaster was missing from his cheek, exposing dark bruises and a line of raw stitches. He sucked in smoke and coughed before glancing back at her. His voice was slurred. "You love that guy, don't you?"

She still wanted to hurt him for what he had done to her that day. "What if I do? What business is it of yours?"

He sucked in smoke again. It was a full ten seconds before he answered her. "He won't marry you, baby. You know that, don't you?"

With her anger was surprise that in his condition he could string words together to make any sense. "He won't if you go on spoiling my chances. Go to bed and leave me alone."

He winced as if in pain. "I haven't spoilt it for you, kid. Honest I haven't. If he'd wanted to marry you, why hasn't he asked you before? He's known you since you were a kid."

With her hopes renewed again, his question only fed her resentment. "What do you know about it? If his father hadn't sent him to America, things would probably have been different. He's never forgotten me. You could see that tonight."

"Who're you trying to convince, baby? You or me?"

The knowledge he could be right added fuel to her anger. "Why don't you go to bed and leave me in peace?"

Rising unsteadily, he approached her bedside instead. "Baby, you're a nice kid. Don't get hurt by this. I don't want that."

31

Her voice struck at him. "Don't get hurt? You act in front of half New York as if you own me and then say don't get hurt?"

His frown was confused. "Yeah. I shouldn't have done that. Only I'm crazy about you, baby, and at the time it seemed the right thing to do."

"Right thing? With every damned newspaper looking for an excuse to link us together? I want you to call a Press Conference tomorrow and announce that we're not engaged and have no intention of getting engaged. Now or ever. Do you hear me?"

His expression told her she had hurt him badly but at that moment she wanted nothing more. Wincing again, he muttered something and retreated to the door. There he turned. "O.K., baby, if that's what you want. But don't fool yourself it'll make any difference to Paul. If you think that, you'll just get hurt all the more."

At that moment she hated him. "Go to bed, for God's sake, and let me get some sleep."

The packet of letters were brought up to the suite the following morning when McArthur was in the bathroom and Delia was waiting to phone Paul. Slipping the rubber band off the package, Delia found four envelopes bearing an Irish forwarding postmark addressed to her. One was from her parents, another from her sister, and a third from Alan Wright. All had to surrender priority to the fourth which was from Paul. With the sense of expectancy his letters always brought her, she sank down on the settee, curled her legs beneath her, and opened the envelope.

She had read no more than a dozen lines when she gave a gasp of shock. As she read on, the luxurious suite seemed to turn deathly quiet and cold. When McArthur came out of the bathroom she was sobbing bitterly. Frowning, he hurried towards her. "What is it, honey? What's happened?"

When she did not answer he saw the letters lying on the nearby table. Noticing the Irish postmark, he showed concern. "It's not bad news from home, is it?"

Turning away, she buried her face in a cushion. When she shook her head, McArthur picked up a handwritten page of Paul's letter that had slipped down to the carpet. He read a few lines, then cursed. "So he's had the guts to tell you at last, has he?"

For a moment his words did not register. Then her tear-stained face turned. "At last? What does that mean? That you knew all the time?"

"What do you think I was trying to tell you last night?"

"But how could you know?"

"Do you think I wasn't curious why Sorenson would do Paul a favour like that? I wrote back straight away to ask. The answer didn't surprise me. I've met Gloria a few times. She usually gets what she wants."

At that moment she felt betrayed by the whole world. "Then why didn't you tell me?"

"Why should I? You never said you were engaged to the guy. It didn't seem any of my business."

"But couldn't you guess how I felt about him?"

"I began to, honey. But what was I supposed to do?"

In her misery she was remembering the times he had tried to make love to her and the reason she had rejected him. "You never thought of the effect it was having on me?"

His bruised face attempted a grin. "It did occur to me once or twice."

"Then why didn't you tell me about this girl?"

He shifted uncomfortably as if embarrassed by his sensitivity. "Maybe I should have done. Only I guess by this time I didn't want to hurt you."

Her surprise at seeing him in this new light was momentarily eclipsed as a fresh spasm of misery ran through her. "Why didn't he tell me before? Why didn't he tell me last night?"

"I don't think he had the guts," McArthur said.

She stared at him angrily. "Paul? A coward? You don't know what you're talking about."

He shrugged. "All right. Maybe he was also afraid of hurting you. Or maybe he didn't know you were still so struck on him after so long. Who knows why people do things?"

Her mind was searching for excuses for him. "Perhaps his father's been putting pressure on him. Didn't you say Sorenson's a senator? Perhaps Sir Richard wants a senator's influence."

Sighing, McArthur dropped on the settee alongside her. "Honey, stop it. That kind of talk gets you nowhere."

She clung to her argument as if it were a lifeline. "I'm sure that's it! His father wanted a daughter-in-law who could further his American interests."

"For Christ's sake, honey, you're making Paul sound like a goddamned puppet now. He's a man. He's old enough to do what he wants."

"No, he doesn't. Otherwise he'd have told me about Gloria before. I just know he would." As pain stabbed her again, she turned and threw herself into his arms. "Oh, Dean, I'm so unhappy. I'm so unhappy I want to die."

He put an arm around her and ran his hand through her blonde hair. "I'm sorry, honey. I just wish I could help."

Beneath his dressing-gown she could feel the strong, steady beat of his heart. She found it comforting and after a moment her sobs eased. She pressed closer to him. "Tell me something, Dean. Weren't you ever tempted to tell me?"

She knew he was grinning. "You mean when I made passes at you? Honey, I used to go away and bang my head against the wall. I told myself I was crazy."

Almost imperceptibly her hand tightened on his arm. "But you never did." A short silence, and then her muffled voice sounded again. "I owe you an awful lot, don't I, Dean?"

He shrugged. "It's worked both ways, honey. I wouldn't be swanning around in New York like this if you hadn't come to my rescue."

She had never heard him talk this way before. In the pause that followed, she felt they were both waiting for the other to speak. She lifted her wet eyes. "I'm sorry I've been so hard on you, Dean. I must have given you a lot of pain."

"A lot of pleasure too, honey. Let's not forget that."

"No. I haven't given you much. Not of myself. I've been very selfish."

If he had taken advantage of her admission, she knew she would have given herself to him but it would have stopped there. Instead he shrugged again. "We are what we are, baby. I've never blamed you."

Again her voice was muffled by his dressing-gown. "I like you, Dean. You're a flirt, you can be big-headed and arrogant, and you drink far too much. But I've still grown to like you."

"You have? That sounds like progress, baby."

She knew that after all she had said to him the previous night she would have to make the first move. "Did you really mean what you said on the parade? You weren't still drunk, were you?"

"Drunk? I'd a goddamned hangover. I'd never been more sober in my life."

"You meant it even though you knew all about me and Paul?"

"Yeah. Why not?"

"So things haven't changed between us this morning?"

He drew back so that he could see her expression. "What are you saying, baby? Would I still ask you to marry me? If you are, the answer's yes. Yes, yes, yes!"

Unable to meet his eyes, she buried her face again. "It sounds terrible, I know. As if I'm coming to you on the rebound. Do you mind that?"

His big, jubilant laugh rang round the suite. "Honey, I don't give a damn what the reason is. Just say yes: that's all I want." When she nodded jerkily, his arms almost squeezed the breath from her body. "Baby, that's stupendous! Are you going to tell Paul?"

"Yes. But I don't want to see him."

"O.K. Do it over the phone. What about the Press Conference? Can we forget about that too?"

Without knowing why she was crying again, she shook her head. "No, you can still call it. But this time you can tell them we're getting married."

SIX

They were married a week later in a New York registry office. The two publishers, to whom Delia and McArthur had given their life stories in the breathing space after the ticker-tape parade, wanted maximum publicity. Delia, for reasons of her own, wanted a small private affair, to be followed by a honeymoon train ride across the States to California so that she could see more of the country that had taken her to its heart.

Although the two newspapers had to agree, there was no way to stop them leaking out the news. The honeymoon couple had no sooner stepped out on the steps of the registry office when thousands of well-wishers surged forward to deluge them with confetti. With hysteria creating hysteria like a fire feeding on itself, it took over twenty burly policemen to protect and usher them away.

If there had ever been a danger of their flight becoming a nine-day wonder, it was dispelled that afternoon when the first editions appeared on the newstands. AIR ACES MARRY; FLYING HEROES TIE KNOT; HAPPY LANDINGS DEAN AND DELIA, were but a few of the hundreds of banner headlines on both sides of the Atlantic. McArthur, now fully recovered from his injuries and jubilant over his marriage, took it all in his stride. "Honey, this is going to double sales when our life stories come out and that'll double our publicity value. The sky's the limit now, baby."

They left on their continental journey that same night, travelling in a special coach the railway company had laid on for them. To Delia it sometimes seemed as if the rest of the train was occupied by pressmen rather than the public for as soon as they moved from their coach cameras flashed and reporters jostled round them.

A similar reception awaited them at every stop along the way. Although New York's hysteria had infected all Americans, until now they had been able to see the famous couple only on cinema newsreels. Now, with them travelling across the entire breadth of the vast country, it was an opportunity too good to miss. Along the entire catchment area that flanked the rail track, automobiles poured in. Enterprising bus companies studied timetables and ran coaches to synchronize with stopping places. Faced by such interest, the railway company re-wrote the train's schedules by making its whistle-stops longer and more frequent.

It made honeymooning difficult for the couple because some of these stops were in the middle of the night. Nevertheless they never failed to appear on the open caboose that the company had hitched on the rear of the train. Resigned that their honeymoon had turned into a national event, they had both decided to make the most of it and gain all the goodwill they could.

After her letter from Paul, Delia was surprised to find her honeymoon was happier than she had imagined. In spite of all the ballyhoo, there were hours when she and McArthur were alone in the luxurious coach and she found him much more attentive and thoughtful than his earlier behaviour had hinted. He drank moderately, he ensured she was given every comfort by the railway staff, and he made love to her with a pleasing mixture of passion and consideration. Although she knew he owed his sexual expertise to the many women he had known, she was honest enough to admit it made no difference to the physical pleasure he gave her. With America sliding in its vastness past the windows, with crowds reminding her at every stop of the celebrity she had become, and with McArthur making love to her in both the sunlit and the moonlit hours, the journey took on a dreamlike quality, one she was to look back on later as a nostalgic interlude between one turbulent period of her life and the next.

All too soon they crossed the Rockies and reached California. After another wild reception in Los Angeles where, to Delia's great excitement, she found dozens of Hollywood's most famous film stars queuing up to meet them, they were driven to a holiday villa on the Santa Barbara coast.

The villa, built on stilts above the beach, was owned by the oil company who had provided the fuel and some of the expenses for McArthur's Atlantic attempt. It existed to provide free, luxurious holidays for the company's executives, but because of the publicity McArthur was now receiving, those same directors had voted it could be used by the flier and his young wife until ambition drove them on.

With company guards provided to ensure privacy, it was a honeymooner's paradise. The sandy beach below belonged to the estate and was extensive enough to keep curious spectators at bay. For the first few days the couple spent their time sun-bathing, swimming in the warm Pacific, reading reviews of their achievements, and making love in the balmy, semi-tropical nights. It was a diversion that recuperated jaded minds and weary bodies and for Delia it dispelled at last the memory of her ordeal in fog and the Bellanca's final crash.

It was an idyllic life but because of the personalities of the couple not one that could last long. Delia, perhaps because she was the younger, was the first to feel the stir of ambition again.

At first it came only as a vague restlessness. She had felt it before when on holiday in England. After a few days of doing nothing she would feel almost a sense of guilt. When she had mentioned it to Alan Wright, he had told her in his wry way that it was a disease endemic to Northerners. "It's the Puritan thing, love. They brainwashed us into believing it's a sin not to work. That's why your unemployed Northerner is such a gloomy character."

It was not a sensation she welcomed. Having denied herself physical sex for so long, she was revelling in McArthur's skilful love-making and there was pain in the thought of tearing herself away from their sybaritic life and entering the harsh, competitive world again. Yet as one warm autumn week slipped into the next, a sense of self-betrayal began to infect her.

It was aided and abetted by the articles they were receiving daily from the press-cutting agency. Now that the initial euphoria of their flight had died, responsible magazines and aviation journals were beginning to make more sober assessments of their achievement and its implications.

Although at first these articles remained full of respect for the couple, they devoted much more space to their in-flight problems. Some were nearer the truth than others, but Delia noticed one thing was common to them all: they were based on the assumption that McArthur had been the key figure throughout. It had been he who had taken all the decisions, he who had navigated, he who had taken over the aircraft during emergencies. Even when she had taken his place at the controls, the assumption was always that she had flown under his surveillance. All these articles, she noted, were written by men.

Before her marriage she would have made bitter and aggressive comment on the sexist bias of the articles. Now, with a large part of her still enjoying the novelty of marriage, she was less eager to raise issues that might, however slightly, change the idyllic pattern of her life.

Consequently it was in the middle of the third week, when her nascent restlessness could no longer be ignored, that she allowed one of these issues to disturb her. If no denial were made to this seemingly universal belief that she had played only a minor role in the flight, then in spite of all the rapturous acclaim given her, she would be little better off in obtaining sponsors for a solo flight than she had been back in England. She made the point as delicately as possible to McArthur one afternoon when they were lying on the beach after a swim.

"Darling, have you noticed how all these articles we get suggest I played second fiddle to you throughout the flight?"

The question appeared to surprise him. "No. Do they?"

"Of course they do. Some of them make me seem little more than a passenger."

He pushed a grape into her mouth, then took one himself. With his bruises gone, his beard almost regrown, and his long, powerful body tanned by the Californian sun, he looked a hundred per cent fitter than the man she had met in London. "I shouldn't worry about it, honey. You know what those guys are like. They write anything that suits 'em."

"Yes, but they're doing me damage, aren't they? If everyone believes them, how am I going to get sponsors when I plan my solo flight?"

He stared at her. "When you what?"

"When I make my next flight. I can't leave it too long. People soon forget."

He looked both puzzled and amused. "Honey, you're married now. Have you forgotten?"

"What's that got to do with it?"

"What's that to do with it? Marriage means babies. You want a baby, don't you?"

She hesitated. "Of course I do. But not yet. I want to establish my career first."

He looked genuinely puzzled now. "But, honey, you've made your name. You're headline news in every newspaper in the world. What more do you want?"

She found it hard to believe that he could not understand. "I'm headline news because I'm the first woman to make an east-west crossing. I'm headline news because people believe I was your assistant. But I'm not headline news as a woman solo flier. And that's what I want to be."

For a moment she feared he was going to laugh at her. Then his expression changed. "I know you've always been ambitious. But can't that wait a while? You're enjoying yourself, aren't you?"

She was only too eager to reassure him. "Yes. I couldn't be happier."

"Then why rush things? You're still a kid: you've plenty of time. Have a baby first and then think about it."

She was dismayed. Although physically inexperienced before her marriage, she had learned all about contraceptive devices from her sister and McArthur's use of them had convinced her that he was in no more of a hurry for a child than she was.

She said as much to him now. "You never said you were keen to start a family."

"I guess we've never got round to it yet. But I would like a kid, honey. There are times when I miss Peter."

"But surely your ex-wife must let you see him?"

"It's not that easy in this country when people live so far apart. Anyway, it only seems to unsettle the boy when he spends a few days with me."

She knew she ought to be glad to discover he had such feelings. At the same time they seemed to put her in the wrong. "We'll have a baby, Dean. But, as you say, there's plenty of time. Let me first make my name as a solo flier. It's important to me for all kinds of reasons."

He eyed her curiously. "What reasons?"

"First for myself. It's been my ambition since I was a child. But I also want to do it for my sex. I want men to see that women are capable of doing more than having babies and cooking meals."

He laughed aloud. "Honey, that's bullshit. Women like it the way they are. And so do men. Why try to rock the boat?"

She bit her lip. "It's not bullshit to me. I hate being treated like a second-class citizen."

His amusement grew. "Who's ever treated you that way? Tell me."

"These articles do. I know and you know that I did a man's job on that flight. But that's not what these articles are saying. They're making out I played the usual role of a woman, the assistant to the man, the secretary to the boss. And that's unfair, isn't it?"

It was an accusation he could hardly deny. "So what do you want, honey? To do your solo flight first and then have a baby?" When she nodded: "O.K. I'd better agree or I'll get no peace. Only don't be too long about it, will you?"

Relieved, she threw herself into his arms. "No. I won't. You're sweet, Dean. I promise I won't keep you waiting too long."

They walked back to the villa a few minutes later and made love. She wondered afterwards if it was because they wanted to lose sight of the small dark cloud on the horizon.

SEVEN

It was towards the end of their third week at the villa that two events occurred to bring the distant storm-cloud a degree nearer, although neither of them suspected it at the time.

One was a long article in *Aviation News*, a specialist West Coast magazine. Written by a well-known ex-flier who had served in France during the war, its acerbic tone was in marked contrast to those that had preceded it. Why, it implied, had the Atlantic east to west crossing been necessary in the first place? It was already known that the Wright Whirlwind engine could run for forty hours and more without maintenance: it was equally obvious that no sane fare-paying passenger was going to cross the Atlantic squashed in the tiny cabin of a Bellanca. Then what had the flight proved? Only that some people would go to any lengths for publicity. Had the McArthurs never paused to think that instead of advancing the cause of aviation they would have set it back for years had they plunged into the sea to their deaths?

It was an article that had infuriated both fliers, particularly when Jimmy Carlile, now back in New York, had phoned to say a syndicated version had appeared in the *New York Times*. "I thought you'd better know, Mac, in case you want to reply. But don't let it worry you. It's just goddamn sour grapes. If you'd landed in Los Angeles instead of New York they'd be purring over you like a cat with cream."

After consultation, Delia and McArthur penned a joint reply, making the point that when the public realized a tiny plane like the Bellanca could span the Atlantic their confidence in larger aircraft must be greatly increased. It was printed in the *Aviation News* without further comment but the incident served to remind both fliers that pioneer flying was not without its enemies.

The second event happened one evening when the two of them were leaving a convention of film producers and directors, where they had been invited to talk. As they entered the parking lot, a man jumped out of a car and approached them.

"Mac, I'd like a word with you. O.K.?"

McArthur swung around. His tone told Delia at once that he knew the man and disliked him. "Hooper! What do you want?"

The man was tall and gaunt, with hollow cheeks, a lantern jaw, and steel-rimmed glasses. To Delia he looked like a downbeat version of Abraham Lincoln. Ignoring McArthur's hostility, he turned to Delia. "Good evening, Mrs McArthur. Sorry to disturb you like this but I only saw the transcript of your interview with Morgan this morning. I did phone you earlier but I guess you were out."

A sudden premonition twinged Delia like a decaying tooth. Her glance at her husband forced McArthur to introduce them. "It's Matt Hooper of the *Los Angeles Times*, honey. I think they call him an investigative journalist."

Although his contempt was barely concealed, Hooper gave no evidence of it. "Mac and I are old friends, Mrs McArthur. Underneath our rugged exteriors, we've a lot of respect for one another."

McArthur's voice was aggressive. "We were on our way home, Hooper. What do you want?"

The journalist glanced down at a notebook he was carrying. "It's related to your injuries before your Atlantic flight, Mac, and the pain-killers you had to take. Morgan asked you if you'd had to take a heavy dose before take-off. You said you'd no option, otherwise you couldn't lift your arm to the throttle. Right?"

To Delia, McArthur's hostile expression was betraying him. "I don't remember. It's some time since the interview."

"You did, Mac. It's in the transcript." Hooper glanced at his car. "You want to see it?"

"No. O.K., I said it. So what?"

Hooper glanced at his notes again. "At this point your wife broke in and said the two of you had made a deal beforehand to share the flying."

Delia nodded as the journalist's eyes moved to her. "That's true. We did."

Hooper turned back to McArthur. "Morgan then said what your wife really meant was that sometimes you went without pain-killers so that you could keep awake. Isn't there something inconsistent there?"

"What do you mean – inconsistent?"

"You'd said earlier you couldn't reach the throttle without pain-killers. Yet your wife said you went without them so you could take your share of the flying. How come?"

Delia broke in quickly. "That's easily explained. Once you're airborne and flying at cruising speed, you don't need to touch the throttle very often. If Dean had to, he could reach it with his right arm."

"But what about the stick?"

"It's possible to hold it with one's legs for a short time. Or Dean could brace it with his injured arm. Lifting the arm was his main problem."

Behind his spectacles, the journalist's sharp eyes were missing nothing. "So you're still saying Mac shared the flying all the way over?"

McArthur's face turned dark with anger. "What the hell does that mean? Are you saying I didn't?"

"No. I'm just trying to figure out how you did it, Mac. It's hard for a dumb guy like me to see how anyone in the pain you were in could keep going for forty hours. Not without drugs, that is. And if you'd taken drugs all that time, you'd have been in no shape to fly. Right?"

McArthur took an aggressive step forward. "Then you're calling both of us liars?"

Alarmed at the way the interview was going, Delia grabbed his arm. "Mr Hooper's only doing his job, Dean."

He threw off her hand. "A hell of a job. Muck-raking to cause trouble."

Steeled by a hundred similar encounters, the lean Hooper did not bat an eyelid. "Sorry, Mac, but your wife's right. To me those statements don't match. I came to find the answer."

"Well, you've got your goddamned answer. Not just from me but from my wife."

As the journalist glanced at her, Delia nodded. "We shared

it as arranged, Mr Hooper. Equal shifts and equal hours. All the way across."

Although she was certain he did not believe her, Hooper gave her a nod of respect. "Thanks, Mrs McArthur. Can I ask what your future plans are? Do you intend to do more flying?"

McArthur moved forward again. "That's it, Hooper. Your time's up."

Having lied for him, Delia was determined not to lose the opportunity the journalist was giving her. "Yes, of course I do. I'm planning a long-distance solo flight."

He showed immediate interest. "May I ask where to?"

"I haven't finalized it yet. But I thought I might try for the San Diego-Caracas light plane record."

From the corner of her eye, she saw McArthur give a start. Hooper's expression was enigmatic. "Isn't that record held by your husband?"

"Yes, but Dean doesn't mind. He's a good sport."

"Yeah, I'm sure he is." Hooper folded up his notebook. "I must let you folk get back home. Thanks for the interview."

McArthur was already walking away. As Delia gave the journalist a smile and turned to follow McArthur, Hooper held out his hand. "You're quite a woman, Mrs McArthur. Good luck with your plans."

She found McArthur already seated in their car with an open hip flask in his hand. Her heart sank as he turned to her. "Why the hell were you so polite to the sonofabitch? Couldn't you see he was just trying to stir up trouble."

She sank into the seat alongside him. Although it was distressing to put into words, she knew it had to be said. "Dean, you have to face it. You can't stop a journalist or anybody else asking questions if he sees we've been telling lies."

"What the hell do you mean – lies?"

"We did tell lies, didn't we? We didn't share all the flying." When he muttered something and turned away, her tone changed. "I don't mind – I never have – but you mustn't flare into a rage if people see through our story. You only give yourself away."

He took another drink from the flask before turning back to her. "What's all this leading to? Do you want to tell them what happened?"

It was their first quarrel and she was close to tears. "No, of course I don't. I just want you to keep calm if anyone else questions us. They can't prove anything as long as we both keep to our stories."

As he gazed at her, she suddenly realized where their lies had led them. His fame, his entire credibility, lay in her hands. Suddenly frightened, she caught hold of his arm. "Dean, let's stop quarrelling, please. Let's forget we ever saw Hooper. There's nothing he can do to us."

As he continued to gaze at her she felt her muscles tightening. Had it already happened, she wondered? Would he see her as a threat from now on?

He turned away and lit a cigarette. From her tone she knew she was trying to appease him. "You didn't mind my mentioning my solo flight, did you? It seemed too good an opportunity to miss."

His thoughts seemed far away. "Why should I mind? You've already said it was something you wanted to do."

"Yes, but I hadn't mentioned the San Diego-Caracas flight before."

He shrugged. "Why not? It's as good as any."

"Yes, but I wouldn't want to break a record of yours." Realizing what she had said, she went on quickly. "Not that I'd be likely to. But you know what I mean."

He drew in smoke. "Good luck, honey. I hope you make it."

She bit her lip. "All I want to do is prove that a woman can make such a flight. That's all." When he did not answer, she went on: "Afterwards, let's fly together again. A really big flight. Perhaps to the Middle East and back. What do you say?"

He nodded as if not listening. "If you're serious about this Caracas flight, you'll need a new ship. And you'll need to stay in California. Is that what you want?"

"Yes. I think I'd like to stay here through the winter. Wouldn't you?"

"Yeah, why not? Then we'd better start looking for a place next week."

Seeing he was coming out of his mood, she hugged his arm again. "If I decide on the Caracas flight, will you help me with the arrangements?"

He looked surprised by the question. "Yeah, of course. You'll need advice, baby. It's a dangerous trip. You're over jungle most of the way."

She leaned over and kissed him. "You're a terrific sport, Dean. Do you know that?"

He made love to her again that night. He made it with care and consideration as well as passion as if making up for their quarrel. She was luxuriating in the thought when an alien one entered her mind like a cold draught into a room. Could such attention be a bribe to prevent her talking and destroying him?

She knew the suspicion was absurd: he had shown her the same consideration long before Hooper's arrival. It was not, therefore, the substance of the suspicion that kept her awake half the night. It was the fear its reasonless shadow would always appear whenever he gave her a gift or performed an act of love.

EIGHT

They set up house in a large rented villa in Roxbury Drive. Delia had wanted a smaller house but McArthur felt differently and she soon understood why. In his one-time role of playboy he had cultivated acquaintances from all walks of society. These celebrities and their hangers-on had tended to abandon him during the days of his decline but now that he was famous again, they were only too pleased to attend the extravagant parties he began to throw.

Delia felt she could not object. With her intention of attempting a record-breaking solo flight giving her constant publicity while McArthur was showing no inclination to attempt one himself, his parties seemed the only vehicle that could keep his name in the newspapers. Moreover he had given way to her on the dual flight that he wanted and had promised to help her in every way on her solo venture. To deny him the parties that he enjoyed seemed ungrateful.

At the same time the cost of all this high living worried her because she felt obliged to contribute her share towards it. As a consequence the *New York Times* money, which she had intended to keep as a nest egg, was diminishing at an alarming rate.

A further concern to her was McArthur's behaviour. Since their interview with Hooper, he had commenced drinking again and although he would take some notice of her when she begged him to drink less, all would be forgotten the moment he was back with his friends again.

Feeling that another dual record attempt might have saved him from this endless round of parties and high living, she wished at times she had agreed to it but on every occasion her ambition overruled her. She had already allowed him to take the major credit for the flight she had virtually made on her own. If they flew together again, the same thing would happen. She had to prove she was a capable pilot in her own right or all the fame she had won would be a mockery of her ambition.

She was also beginning to think that another dual flight would be bad for McArthur. However he behaved towards the world, he must know he had failed her during those last twenty hours of stress and danger. More and more the conviction was growing in her that the very flight that had brought him renewed fame had damaged further his confidence to fly solo and the heavy drinking and extravagant parties were evidence of this. Only a successful solo flight would restore his confidence and at every opportunity she encouraged him to attempt one. His answer was always the same. Good idea, baby, but not yet. There's plenty of time ...

Not that she was finding it easy to make her own plans. The many articles that, intentionally or not, had given the impression McArthur had been the key figure during the flight proved to have done their damage when she searched for sponsors. Her name was enough to gain her interviews and, aided by her femininity, to ensure she was wined and dined as a celebrity. But when the matter of individual sponsorship was raised, the excuses were many and varied but all meant the same. If she flew with McArthur the help would be there. If she tried to fly alone, it would not.

It was a situation that brought out every dogged element in her nature. One way or another, even if it meant spending every penny saved from her Atlantic flight, she would prove to the world she was a record-breaking flier in her own right.

Eight more weeks of effort and disappointment followed. Although between parties and McArthur's bouts of drinking her marriage still brought her happiness, self-honesty made her admit there were moments when she felt resentment towards him. It was not so much the promise he had wrung from her before the flight that she resented: it was the fact he had taken no steps afterwards to refute the general belief he had been the key figure during it. Sometimes she felt that if he had even acknowledged to her in private that her present difficulties were due to this misconception, she could have forgiven him. But he seemed totally unaware of it and with every new failure to obtain sponsorship her resentment grew. Afraid of it, she threw herself into love-making with an almost frenzied zeal, ironically making him believe their relationship was deepening.

However, her resentment was not one-sided. Towards the end of the ninth week, one of McArthur's friends paid him a visit in the late afternoon. As the two of them moved towards his liquor cabinet, she spotted a late edition newspaper left by the visitor on a chair. Picking it up, she was idly paging through it when a large photograph on the centre page struck her like a blow in the face. Above it was a caption. MARRIAGE OF THE MONTH. GLORIA SORENSON MARRIES SON OF ENGLISH EARL.

She fled with the paper into her room. Before she finished reading the double column paragraph beneath the photograph, tears were streaming down her cheeks.

Her distress made no sense to her. She had known for months about Paul's engagement, and even though some childlike creature within her had whispered he could never marry anyone but herself and something would happen to stop him, she had steeled herself for this day. Yet now it had come, she felt as if her heart would break.

She was still sobbing when McArthur entered the room fifteen minutes later. "What is it, baby? What's happened?"

Realizing she had left the newspaper open beside her she tried to cover it with her arm. As he jerked the paper away and stared at it, she heard him curse.

With her face still buried in the pillow, she reached an arm back to him. At that moment she wanted nothing more but to throw herself into his arms and find comfort there. Instead there was a long silence. Lifting her head, she turned to him, only for him to throw the newspaper back on the bed and walk from the room. A moment later she heard the clink of bottles and the pouring of liquid.

Another month passed in which would-be sponsors made reassuring noises but did nothing else. Although McArthur's extravagances had more than halved her savings, she was considering buying a light aircraft for herself when she remembered Hooper of the *Los Angeles Times*. On an impulse she phoned him and asked for an interview. His response was immediate. "Where, Mrs McArthur? At your home or in my office?"

"I'll come and see you. When would suit you?"

"How about tomorrow morning? Around eleven?"

"Yes, thank you. That'll suit me fine."

She arrived early but was taken immediately to his office. To reach it she was led across the main floor of the building, a sea of hurrying messengers, clacking typewriters, and ringing telephones. Hooper was waiting for her outside his office. Although his gaunt angled face with his steel-rimmed glasses gave nothing away, she felt he was pleased to see her as he shook hands and led her to a well-worn armchair. "Would you like a cup of coffee, Mrs McArthur?"

She gave him a smile. "Yes, thank you. I would."

He returned to the office door to call back his assistant. While he was occupied, her eyes took in his office. A battered typewriter, trays of papers, and a telephone stood on the plain desk before her. Two metal filing cabinets rested against the walls. The only evidence provided by the office of the journalist's importance were the many framed photographs that lined the walls. Although some faces were unknown to her, she recognized members of the British royal family, well-known politicians on both sides of the Atlantic, and current stars of both stage and screen. As some were autographed, she guessed they were all celebrities he had personally interviewed.

Half a minute later Hooper lowered his lean body into the chair behind the desk. "Coffee might take a few minutes. Do you want to talk now or wait for it?"

She was feeling nervous. "I'd rather talk. I don't want to take up too much of your time."

He nodded. "O.K. What can I do for you?"

Although as far as her sponsorship problems were concerned, she had decided to take him into her full confidence, the knowledge she was asking for his help embarrassed her and she finished with a diffident laugh. "It's absolutely ridiculous. I'm known wherever I go; I can go into almost any store in the country and get unlimited credit; and yet when I ask someone to sponsor the very thing that got me all this publicity and ballyhoo they make every noise but the right one.''

His gimlet eyes had not moved from her face, making her wonder at the thoughts behind them. "Don't tell me you don't know why, Mrs McArthur.''

Resentment made her reply stronger than she had intended. "I know why all right. It's all these damned sexist articles that automatically assume Dean did all the hard work and took all the decisions. Whereas, as we've both said from the beginning, it was a joint effort.''

He picked up a pencil from his desk, examined it for a moment, then raised his eyes again. "Are you looking for my advice, Mrs McArthur?''

She hesitated. "Yes, I suppose I am.''

"Then why don't you tell the truth about your flight?''

She stiffened. Although she knew of his suspicions, she had never expected to hear them put as bluntly as this. Her voice turned cold. "What do you mean by that?''

"You know very well what I mean. Mac never played his part on that flight. I guessed that right away when I read Morgan's transcript, and you gave yourself away when I interviewed you.''

For a moment she felt panic-stricken. "Where do you get such ideas from? Is it that you don't like my husband?''

He dropped the pencil and looked at her. "We had a fracas once, but that's got nothing to do with this case. I wasn't fooled by your stories, any more than I was fooled by that photograph taken over Nova Scotia with him at the controls. My guess is that he knew a plane would come up and take pictures and so he took over until it flew away. Aren't I right?''

His words confirmed an old suspicion and turned her hot and cold. "No, you're not. We flew two hours on and two hours off right through the flight. Why can't you believe us like everyone else does?''

He shrugged. "People believe what they want to believe, Mrs McArthur. Most of them want to believe the man is the leader and the woman his assistant. Hence your sexist articles. You're never going to tip the scales and achieve your ambition unless you tell the truth. It's as simple as that.''

Fear that he was right and apprehension what the interview

might lead to made her strike at him. "You're right that people believe what they want to believe. You've no proof Dean didn't play his part but because you don't like him, you've convinced yourself he didn't. Isn't that true?"

"It's true I've no proof yet, Mrs McArthur. But it's only fair to tell you I've got a man over in Ireland doing some research for me. Maybe he'll find the proof I want."

Panic-stricken now, she could not for the moment decide whether there was evidence in Ireland or not. "Why are you doing this? Why do you want to cause trouble to both of us?"

He leaned forward. "Two reasons, Mrs McArthur. I'm a professional journalist and my job is to ferret out the truth no matter who it hurts. The second reason's more personal. I think it's a goddamned shame your ambitions have to suffer because McArthur's taking the credit for your guts and skill."

She had another fear now, that his condemnation of McArthur was chipping at the very fabric of her marriage. "But he's not taking credit. He's said time and time again that I did as much as he did."

"Knowing all the time that people think he's just being chivalrous? You think that's the best he can do?"

His contempt brought her to her feet. "You're not being fair to him. He can't be blamed how people interpret the things he says."

He rose with her. "Maybe. Maybe not. But before you go, there's something I want you to believe. I admire you, Mrs McArthur, both for your achievement and your loyalty. So while I'm waiting to hear from Ireland, I intend writing an article saying how short-sighted business institutions are in not sponsoring you. I'm not promising it'll clear the way for you but it might help."

"I'm not interested," she said tightly. "I don't want your help."

He lifted an eyebrow. "But isn't that what you came for?"

She was near to tears. "If it was, it shows what a damn fool I am, doesn't it? I think you're contemptible trying to stir up trouble like this."

His shrug was a blend of sarcasm and regret. "A journalist's lot, Mrs McArthur. Believe it or not, I still wish you well and hope you prove the pundits wrong."

"Go to hell," she said, walking out. It was only when she was in the cab that was taking her home that her temper began to cool and she was able to think rationally.

Her first sensation was relief. Try as she would, she could think of nothing that had happened in Ireland to incriminate McArthur. Their deal had been made in secret and providing she kept her mouth closed in the days ahead, Hooper could prove nothing.

Her second thought was less reassuring. Until today she had seen a personal solo flight simply as a way of establishing her own flying credentials. Now, because of Hooper, she saw it in a different light. So far the pundits had given McArthur most of the credit for her achievements. But if she proved to the world she was as capable as he, would not those same pundits then turn on McArthur and punish him for their own sexist prejudices?

Until now she had fought for sponsors believing success would raise her status while in no way diminishing his. Now that she realized the implications, it would no longer be possible for her to pursue those ambitions without knowing she was putting Dean's well-being at risk. Not for the first time that day she damned the impulse that had led her to Hooper's office.

NINE

Hooper's article appeared three days later and was syndicated throughout the States. As he had promised, it castigated the faint-heartedness of business institutions for not putting faith in a girl who had shown such courage and flying skill on a mission that had taken aviation a giant step forward. It also condemned the experts for their sexist bias in giving most of the credit to McArthur.

Its first fruit was not auspicious. Uncertain how McArthur would react and seeing no point in stirring up trouble if the article never appeared, Delia had not so far mentioned her interview. Now, on seeing the half-page article in the morning edition, she knew the issue had to be faced.

It was well past eleven o'clock when McArthur emerged from the bathroom. Although he had bathed and was wearing a bathrobe, his rugged face was still unshaven and his eyes were red-rimmed. He had been drinking with friends the previous evening and was clearly suffering a hangover.

"Do you want any breakfast?" she asked him.

He grimaced. "No, thanks, honey. Where's the newspaper?"

Feeling stiff with tension she handed the paper to him. It was an effort to keep her voice casual. "Hooper's done an article on me. He seems to think it's unfair I haven't had any sponsors so far."

He gave a start. "Hooper? What the hell's he up to?"

Unintentionally her voice hardened. "He's not up to anything. He just thinks I'm not getting a fair deal."

He glanced at her, then read the article. When his eyes lifted to her, they were hostile. "You've been to see him, haven't you? Why didn't you tell me?"

She fought down her apprehension. "I've been seeing lots of people recently. I didn't think it was that important."

"Hooper? Come on, baby, you can do better than that. Who fixed the interview? You or him?"

"I did," she admitted.

He cursed. "Why?"

"I had the feeling he was sympathetic and might help me. What's wrong with that?"

"What's wrong with it? Can't you see what he's hinting at right through this article? That you did all the work and I got all the gravy. Is that what you wanted?"

The unfairness of his question fired her temper. "There's nothing wrong with him putting up a case for me. Someone has to or I'll never get any sponsors."

To her dismay she could see suspicion in his eyes. "Hooper hates my guts. I told you that at the beginning. Yet he's the guy you went to see. Why?"

She made a last effort to control herself. "He's the one newspaperman who thinks I'm getting a raw deal. And, damn it, I am. I'm amazed you can't see that."

"A raw deal? Famous all over the world! All the clothes and jewellery you can wear! For Christ's sake, what do you want, baby? Buckingham Palace?"

"No. I want what I've always wanted. To be recognized as a flier in my own right. And that's the one thing none of you will give me."

"So you went to Hooper to set the record straight. Is that what you're saying?"

At that her temper exploded. "My God, how dare you say that? After all the lies I've told for you. How dare you!"

Shivering with anger, she did not notice his expression turn into shame. Running from the room, she slammed the door and then burst into tears.

They made love that night. With each of them relieved to be accepted by the other, their embraces were passionate and both were near exhaustion when they finally sank back side by side.

"I'm sorry I was so rough on you, honey. I guess I'm just worried about Hooper, that's all."

"I know you are," she whispered. "But you needn't be. He can't harm us."

"I wish I were as sure as you. I can't help thinking about that guy of his in Ireland."

"What can he find out? There was only you and me in my room when we planned the flight. No one can prove anything if we both keep to our story."

He lifted his head and kissed her. "Yeah, that's true. I'm sorry, kid. I guess I was still half canned from last night."

Like all reconciliations between lovers it was full of warm and penitent relief and as the purple darkness closed in, encapsulating them in time and space, it was easy for each to believe that the doubts and fears that had separated them earlier had no more significance than a summer storm.

The second fruit of Hooper's article came four days later. It was a letter from Paul from Philadelphia. Discovering it in the letter box before McArthur was awake, she took it into her dressing-room to read.

Its contents astonished and excited her. Paul had read Hooper's article and thought it disgraceful that no one had come forward to sponsor her. Accordingly he had approached his father who, after Paul's wedding, had stayed on a while in America to attend to his business interests. Delia was not only English, Paul had pointed out, she was also a product of Brook Lane, and it seemed only right that sponsorship should come from those who had benefited from her achievement.

Sir Richard had made his usual chauvinistic complaints but had finally agreed to give help on the condition her solo flight should take place in the British Empire and not in America. If she accepted this condition, the flight could take place at a date of her own choosing.

Sir Richard had sailed for England that same week but had left him, Paul, to settle the details. He would be in San Francisco on business the following week and he could meet her on either the Thursday or the Friday in Los Angeles. His hotel would be the Ambassador. If she agreed to meet him there, would she please cable him a time and date and he would make the necessary arrangements.

With her heart pounding with excitement, Delia's first

impulse was to rush to McArthur and tell him the news. Then she paused. Dean was jealous of Paul. If she told him at this point of time and he objected to her receiving help from Paul, she would either have to refuse that help and see her ambition die or have an open confrontation with him. Better to see Paul first and learn all the details before breaking the news.

Instead she read the letter over and over. She told herself the only reason for her joy was the possibility she might at last achieve her ambition. But she found it hard to deny that the exaltation it gave her was enhanced and gilded by the knowledge Paul cared enough about her to put that ambition within reach.

TEN

Paul was waiting for her in the foyer of the Ambassador the following Thursday morning. Although she had tried to discipline herself in the cab, her heart gave its familiar impulsive throb when she caught sight of him. Angry with herself, she could find no other defence than a posture bordering on coolness as he approached her.

"Hello, Paul. How nice to see you again."

He took her hands in his. As always she was struck by his youthful appearance and good looks. "Hello, Smudge. May I have a kiss?"

She offered him her cheek. Once again the kiss he planted seemed to burn her skin like fire. Afraid to think of the implications she allowed him to remove her coat.

His dark eyes moved over her admiringly as a girl took the coat from him. She had bought her slim-fitting emerald dress specially for their meeting, using as her excuse the good news he was bringing her. "You look marvellous, Smudge. They wouldn't recognize you back home if they saw you now."

She gave a laugh as she sat down. "Does that mean you weren't impressed by the girl back there?"

"No. I thought she was delightful. But you've grown up since then."

At that moment she wondered if she had. Sitting there with him, listening to his beautifully-modulated English voice, the years seemed to roll back and she could believe herself with him in the Moorland Club when all her romantic dreams were still alive.

She crushed back her sense of disorientation. They were different people today: their stars had separated. To be safe she must talk only about the offer he had made her.

"It's very kind of you to think about me, Paul. I want you to know how much I appreciate it."

He ordered coffee, then turned back to her. "I've wanted to do it for years but I knew my old man would never agree to help a woman unless you had some success under your belt." ·

"Then he does believe I did my part during the flight?"

He laughed. "He put up a bit of a fight. He's still got this thing about women. But that article undoubtedly tipped the scales. How do you feel about his offer?"

Now they were discussing flying, she felt safe. "I'm thrilled. Who wouldn't be? I was beginning to think I'd flown the Atlantic for nothing."

"Then you won't mind making your flight in the Empire instead of in America?"

"Not a bit. I stayed here because everyone's been so kind and made a fuss over me and because Dean's an American. But if I can get sponsorship from Britain, that's all the better."

"What about Dean? Have you spoken to him yet?"

"No. I felt it better to get all the details first."

"You don't think he'll mind your going back to England to make the flight?"

"I don't know. He might or he might not."

"What will you do if he objects?"

She hesitated. "That's a difficult question. But Dean's a flier himself and he'll know what this means to me. I don't think he'll put any real obstacles in my way."

He nodded. "Good. Have you thought yet what record you'll go for?"

"Yes. I'd like to try the London-Cape Town light plane record."

"Would you mind flying in a British aircraft? Dad was very strong on that."

"Not a bit. As I'm English I'd rather fly in one. If he's agreeable I'd use a Puss Moth. I've flown one before. Naturally we'd make sure his tyres and other products got full mention."

Paul laughed. "Don't worry. Father won't forget the finer points. He's too good a business man."

As their coffee arrived she realized that so far they had made no mention of his marriage. Was he avoiding it, she wondered, or was she?

He was pulling a flask from his hip pocket. At her comment he smiled. "Everybody does it now. Prohibition's become a farce. You'll have a drop in your coffee, won't you? It's very good brandy."

"Why not?" she said.

The minutes slipped past like seconds. As they talked more about her flight and she drank a second brandy-laced coffee, her earlier diffidence began to fall away. Why should she not talk about his marriage and about Gloria? He would probably think it strange if she did not.

"How are you finding married life, Paul? Do you like it?"

What was that fleeting look in his eyes, she wondered. Embarrassment? "Very much, thank you. Gloria's looking forward to meeting you. Perhaps she'll get the chance now that father's prepared to sponsor you."

Yet she had not been invited to their marriage, she thought. "Why? Does it mean you'll both come over to England?"

"No, I didn't mean that. I was thinking this sponsorship programme might give you cause to visit us sometime."

She made no comment. An odd recklessness had now taken the place of her diffidence. "Would you come over to England, Paul? Just to see me off?"

His glance defied analysis. "Why? Would you like me to?"

"Oh, yes. It would mean so much …" Then, realizing what she had said: "It would make sense, wouldn't it? With your father behind the attempt?"

He hesitated, then smiled. "I suppose it would. But let's wait and see how things turn out, shall we?"

She wanted to reach across the table and kiss him. Dean had been wrong about him. It was circumstances that had been to blame. His dispatch to America, their long separation, the pressure by his father to make a marriage beneficial to his interests, these were the factors that had come between them. His failure to tell her about Gloria was evidence not of his weakness but of the love he still had for her. At that moment she had forgotten about her own marriage. Had he asked her, she would have gone up to his room without hesitation and made love to him with all the passion in her being.

It felt like emerging from a warm bath into a draughty room when, an hour later, he glanced at his watch and made a wry face. "I'll have to go in a few minutes, Smudge. I must be back in San Francisco first thing tomorrow morning."

The thought of leaving him was painful. "Must you? Couldn't we have lunch and you take a later train?"

His smile made her feel she was melting inside. "I'd love to, Smudge. But I've got some hard-headed Yankee businessmen to meet and I've already put them off once to come here. I can't do it a second time."

She remembered little about their parting except the kiss he gave her before she entered her cab. It was only on her way home that remorse began to enter her thoughts. She had married McArthur; she had enjoyed his love-making during their honeymoon and in the months since; she had even believed she had fallen in love with him and grown alarmed that the lies they had told about the flight might come between them. Yet she had only been in Paul's company for a few minutes when her body had begun crying out for him. If she had committed adultery only with her mind and not with her body, it was only because the opportunity had been lacking. What kind of woman did this make her? Was ambition her only constancy?

It was almost a relief to have another problem to face. With her sponsorship now assured, how should she break the news to Dean? Although he would dislike financial help coming from Paul's family, with none other in view he might just be able to stomach it. But how would he react when told the conditions included her leaving for England?

She glanced at her watch as she stepped out of the cab. It was after two o'clock. Dean would already have had lunch. Perhaps now was the best time to talk to him. Apprehensive, nervous, she slipped the key into the front door of the villa and made for the living-room.

ELEVEN

A vein was standing out on McArthur's neck. "Paul Findlay's father's backing you? In England? Goddamn it, that's too much."

She eyed him in dismay. "Why?"

"Why? Are you saying you don't know?"

"No, I don't know. Paul's father is giving me the chance no one else will give me. What's wrong with that?"

"What do you mean – Paul's father? Why can't you be honest and say Paul?"

"All right – Paul. He's an old friend and wants to help me. Is that a crime?"

His face was dark with jealousy. "There's no way you can shake him out of your hair, is there? Not even after he cheated you over Gloria."

Her temper exploded. "You're a fine one to talk. How many women have you been mixed up with? Ten, fifty, a hundred? What right have you to be jealous over an old friend?"

"Then you admit you've been lovers?"

"No, I don't. But even if we had been, what business would it be of yours? I've been faithful to you ever since we met. Isn't that enough?"

Their quarrel, accentuating the dissipation from his recent excesses, seemed to be ageing him. "Goddamn it, you've just come back from seeing him. Without saying a word to me."

"Do I have to tell you everything I do? I didn't tell you because I knew it would mean a quarrel. And I was right, wasn't I?"

"Why couldn't you have spoken to him on the phone? Why had he to come all the way across the States?"

She made a desperate attempt to bring the quarrel back

under control. "Dean, there's nothing between us. How can there be? Paul's just got married himself. But you can't expect me to turn down his offer. It's obviously the only one I'm going to get."

"I still want to know why he's making it."

Resentment fired her temper again. "It never occurs to you, does it, that some people feel I've had a bad deal and that I'm entitled to a chance to prove myself."

His lips curled. "People like Hooper?"

"Yes, like Hooper. I'm accepting this offer, Dean. And if it means going to England, I'm going. It's my one chance and I'm taking it."

"Hoping all the time Paul will go over as well?"

The knowledge he was right only made her want to hurt him. "My God, you're impossible. I let you take all the credit for the flight and when I get the chance to prove myself, you don't just want to stop me, you try to make it sound dirty as well. Hooper's right. You don't deserve a woman's loyalty."

He stared at her, then cursed. "Jesus Christ! You're really something, baby."

She would have given a year of her life to withdraw the words but it was too late. Turning, he walked away. A few seconds later the front door slammed with a violence that shook the villa to its foundations.

It was after three a.m. when a car came up the drive. From the slurred voices in the doorway a minute later Delia guessed someone had brought Dean home. As the car drove away, she heard his stumbling footsteps in the hall. They made their uncertain way up the stairs and entered the bathroom.

A crash of glass brought her upright in bed. She heard him curse, then the bathroom door opened and his footsteps sounded on the landing again.

Her feelings were confused. One half of her, still smarting from their quarrel, wanted nothing more than to be left alone. Yet the two of them had never slept on a quarrel before and she could not escape the thought that if it happened tonight, it might have a significance beyond the quarrel itself.

She sat listening as he entered his room and heard the protest of springs as he flung himself on the bed. When silence followed she guessed he had fallen asleep fully dressed.

She was tempted to go to him but restrained herself. He was aggressive when drunk and might begin another quarrel. Better to wait until he was sober before attempting a conciliation.

She was trying to sleep when the telephone rang. Startled, she slipped out of bed and ran into the hall. "Hello! Who is it?"

"Is that Mrs McArthur?"

"Yes. Who's that?"

"I'm Sergeant Connors of your local precinct."

Her heart missed a beat. "Yes, Sergeant. What's happened?"

The policeman was clearly embarrassed. "It's about your husband, Mrs McArthur. Has he got home O.K.?"

"Yes, he's in bed. Why?"

"There was trouble tonight in a speakeasy. He was with a friend and got into a fight with two other guys. I had to send men round to break it up."

Her mouth turned dry. "Have you charged him, Sergeant?"

"Naw. The other guys had been on the bottle too. And anyway my men recognized him."

"Was it they who brought him home?" she asked.

"Naw. His friend said he'd take care of him. There is one thing though, Mrs McArthur. He shouldn't have been in a speakeasy. Drinking's still an offence in this state."

"Yes, I know that. I'm sorry, Sergeant."

"Yeah. He'll have to take it easy. The word's getting around. You're following me, Mrs McArthur?"

"Yes, Sergeant. I'll talk to him."

"Yeah. It might be a good idea. Only don't say I phoned you. O.K.?"

"I won't, Sergeant. Thank you for telling me. I appreciate it."

She went into his bedroom a minute later. He was asleep on his side but she could see an abrasion on his left cheek. She removed his shoes and jacket. He groaned, muttered but did not wake up. She then covered him with a quilt and sat in a bedside chair watching him for a few minutes. Finally she switched off the light and went back to her room. Dawn was breaking before she closed her eyes and even then she slept only fitfully.

They made up their quarrel the following afternoon in her room. "Honey, I'm sorry. Only I'm jealous of that guy. I can't help it."

"I know you are. But you don't have to be. He's married now and unless the photographs lie Gloria's a beautiful woman." Before he could comment, she went on: "If I could get sponsorship over here, I wouldn't go. As it is, what choice have I got?"

He ran a hand down her naked back. "You could do that dual flight with me. You'd get plenty of sponsorship for that."

She stiffened involuntarily. "No. I need this flight for myself."

"O.K. But at least let me come with you and help you plan it. It's a big hop, baby. I don't want anything to go wrong."

"No. If you do, they'll take the credit from me again."

"But how can they? You'll still be flying the ship."

"I don't know how but they will. I want to do this myself, Dean, the planning, the aircraft maintenance, everything. And I'll only get credit for it if I do it alone."

She knew how it sounded and she could understand his suspicions. Yet having risked her life once without advancing her cause, she was determined to take no chances this time.

With his bruised face shadowed by the closed curtains, she could not read his expression. When he did not speak, she leaned forward and kissed him. "You will be good while I'm away, won't you?"

His laugh was wry. "You think I might start living the high life again, baby?"

She had already decided to be frank with him about his life style. "You've been living the high life ever since we arrived. I wish you'd ease off on the drinking. It could get you into serious trouble."

"That's just the Puritan in you, honey. Everybody drinks in L.A."

"Not the way you do. But it's not only that. It's your health. You were looking so fit when we were at Santa Barbara."

"And now you think I'm a disaster?"

"Not a disaster, darling. You're still a dreamboat. But you don't look as well as you did."

He grinned. "All the more reason for you to stay and keep me on the straight and narrow."

"But I can't. You drink whether I'm here or not."

"There's one way you could stop me, honey."

"What way?"

"You could have a baby. They say nothing changes a man more than that."

Although she knew he was serious, she decided to treat the comment lightly. "That's blackmail. Anyway, I said we'd have one later on. In the meantime, why don't you start planning another flight?"

"I am planning one. Our next flight together. That's still on, isn't it?"

"Yes, of course it is. As soon as I get back. But I mean one before that. A solo. You'll have no trouble getting sponsors."

"And it would keep me out of mischief, right?"

When in this mood, she had no problem handling him. "Exactly! What about tackling the transcontinental light plane record?"

He shook his head. "If I did anything, I'd go for the L.A.-Alaska hop."

She frowned. "That means another sea flight, doesn't it?"

"It does if you want to break the record. The land route adds on a few hundred miles." His tone changed when he noticed her expression. "What's wrong? You think I can't make it?"

"No, of course I don't," she lied. "But sea flying puts such a heavy reliance on one's aircraft. I don't want to lose you, Dean."

He cuffed her cheek. "Yet you're leaving me to fly to the Cape."

"That's different. You've already proved yourself. I haven't."

He seemed about to say something, then shook his head instead and drew her towards him. She felt like Delilah when she remembered her thoughts about Paul but when he began kissing her, she found her body ignored her guilt. Giving up trying to understand herself, she responded to his love-making with all the zeal and passion of her honeymoon.

She felt as if she was in the middle of a rugby scrum as she and McArthur fought their way to the ship gangway. Cameras were clicking and questions being hurled from all sides. Laughing, unsteady on her high heels and clinging to McArthur's arm, she teetered along the gangway and on to the ship's deck. There, surrounded only by curious passengers, she stood at the rail to allow the cameramen to take a final picture. As a delighted young steward took her grip from McArthur, she gave a last wave and followed McArthur and the boy into a companionway.

They were led with some ceremony into a spacious cabin. As the door closed, McArthur nodded at a bottle of champagne standing on a table and large sprays of flowers lying on the bed. "You don't need a solo flight to the Cape to make you famous, honey. Clara Bow doesn't get a better send-off than this."

She pulled off her hat. "Clara Bow gets it because she's a star in her profession. I get it because I was Dean McArthur's passenger. There's a difference."

"C'mon, honey. It's not as bad as that. Most folks accept you did your share."

She took a cigarette from him. "Most folks not being aviation writers and their kind. Or would be sponsors." Before he could comment, she went on: "Thanks for coming all this way to see me off, Dean. I appreciate it."

He shrugged as he sank down on the bed. "I'd like to be coming a lot further, honey. It's not going to be much fun listening to the news on the radio."

She felt very warm and close to him at that moment. "It's only this once, darling. After this we can go everywhere together."

"Is that a promise, baby?"

She wondered why she hesitated. "Yes, of course it is." She turned to the table. "What about a glass of champagne?"

As she turned with the bottle in her hand, she saw he was reading the cards on the sprays of flowers. Suppressing her resentment, she gave him a smile. "Who're they all from?"

He picked up a large spray of roses. "This one's from Paul

and Gloria. They wish you *bon voyage* and hope to see you in England before you take off." He lowered the spray. "So Paul's not making the trip with you?"

"No. I told you. He has too many commitments at the moment. But he's hoping to bring Gloria over with him on holiday before my flight's due."

He made no further comment but she could sense his relief as he continued sifting through the flowers. "The Mayor of New York, the Chamber of Commerce, the *New York Times* ... you've got some heavy well-wishers, baby." His expression changed as he picked up another spray. "And some sons of bitches too."

She drew nearer. "What does that mean?"

He thrust the large spray at her. "Matt Hooper. Still shooting his goddamned poisoned arrows."

She read the inscription on the card. 'Don't be a fool this time. Keep the credit yourself. Good luck. Matt Hooper.'

She bit her lip as she glanced back at McArthur. "Forget it, Dean. It's just his way."

He drew hard on his cigarette. "Was it he who suggested you shut me out like this? It sounds like the sonofabitch."

With a quarrel the last thing she wanted, she ground out her cigarette, dropped on the bed, and put her arms around him. "Don't start thinking stupid things again, Dean. Not today. Please. Not when I'm going to miss you so much."

She felt him slowly relaxing. "I still wish you'd never gone to see him."

"I know. But he has helped me. So I can't be too angry with him, can I?" When he did not answer, she reached for the champagne again. "Come on, darling. Wish me luck."

He filled two glasses. She held hers out to him. "To both of us, Dean. I'll be back as soon as I can."

"Mind you are, honey. It's going to be lonely over here without you. Particularly at nights."

She smiled and nuzzled against him. "It'll be lonely for me too. But I'll write you often and ring twice a week."

"Yeah, don't forget. And take care of yourself. O.K.?"

"I will," she said, kissing him. "And you do the same. Promise?"

"I promise. Good luck, sweetheart."

The ship edged out into the river fifteen minutes later. Through the streamers thrown by both passengers and well-wishers, she could see his tall figure standing on the quayside. Although conscious of passengers staring at her and whispering, she waved until he merged into the shapeless crowd across the water. Then, feeling intensely lonely, she ran down to her cabin, threw herself down among the flowers, and burst into tears.

TWELVE

It seemed as if the whole of England was in festive mood the day Delia returned home. Southampton, the first town to receive her, was agog with excitement. Bunting and flags fluttered from cranes, a large banner with the caption WELCOME HOME DELIA was draped along one side of the Customs Sheds, a band played popular tunes of the day, and thousands of excited townsfolk lined the quay and the docks. As the *Mauretania* edged towards her berth, tug sirens added to the din and when the gangways clattered into position, excitement rose to fever pitch as spectators pushed forward to gain a better vantage point.

It took a cordon of police to prevent reporters and fans from rushing aboard the ship. When Delia appeared, escorted by half a dozen burly policemen, a cheer went up that sent seagulls soaring high into the air.

The scene when the girl reached the quayside was feverish even on New York standards. Reporters fought to reach her, cameras flashed on all sides, spectators surged forward, and women screamed as they were half-crushed in the mêlée. Trying to keep a smile on her face, Delia was ushered towards a large open-topped limousine. As the rear door opened and she was pushed inside, she heard a wry Yorkshire voice. "It's worse than Hull and Kingston Rovers on Derby Day, isn't it?"

Confused and bewildered by her struggle to reach the car, it took her a moment to identify the speaker. Then she gave a gasp of delight. "Alan! Oh, Alan, how good to see you again."

The forthright Yorkshire engineer showed both pleasure and embarrassment as she threw her arms around him. "Hello, Delia. Welcome home. What's kept you away so long?"

She hugged and kissed him. "Oh, it's good to be back, Alan." Her eyes shone as she gazed at him. "I hadn't realized before how I've missed you all."

Hiding his feelings, Wright said something to the chauffeur, then turned back to her. "We've missed you too. Life's not been the same in the workshop without a woman to gum things up."

She pretended to cuff him and hugged him again instead. Then, as the limousine began to move away, she drew back. "But whose car is it? And where are we going?"

"It's the Old Man's. He sent me down to pick you up. Guess what?"

"What?" she laughed.

"I'm detailed to be your general factotum before and after your Cape Town flight. A sort of engineer-cum-bodyguard-cum-manager. Can you stand it?"

"Stand it? I love it! But what about your work at Brook Lane?"

"Your flight takes priority over it. The Old Man's orders."

"But you can't put your work aside for me. I wouldn't expect it."

He gave her his familiar grin. "It's not what *you* expect. It's what the Old Man expects. Actually, as your Puss Moth's up at Brook Lane and you're likely to be doing your flight trials there, there shouldn't be any problems."

With the slow-moving limousine flanked by cheering spectators, she was forced to share her attention with them. "Where are we going now?" she asked as she waved and blew kisses.

"First to the City Hall to meet the mayor and let the crowds take a good look at you. Then on to London to do the same thing. The BBC want you to do a broadcast tonight, so you've a room booked at the Savoy. After that we drive up to Yorkshire to see your dad and mum and meet the Old Man."

She was showing some dismay. "London? Can't we go straight home?"

They were having to shout now as the limousine turned into a huge crowd outside the dock gates. "They'd feel let down in London if you didn't show up," Wright told her. "They've been lining the streets since early this morning. There's the other angle too. Sir Richard and the other sponsors want you to get all the publicity possible before your Cape flight. I suppose it makes some kind of sense."

"Other sponsors?"

"Yes. The Old Man's got the *Daily Mail* to put some money in. They'd like your exclusive story when you get back. Then there's the de Haviland company, a perfume manufacturer, and a couple of others. So he hasn't a totally free hand in handling your affairs."

A hand banged against the car side and a bunch of dahlias, tied with string, landed on her lap. Turning, she saw a huge red-faced woman beaming and waving at her. Calling her thanks, she glanced back at Wright. "We'll go straight up to Yorkshire after London, won't we? No other stops along the way?"

He gave her a sarcastic grin. "What's the matter? Isn't fame all it's cracked up to be?"

She had forgotten the bluntness of his kind and suddenly realized how much she had missed it. "Fame's all bunkum, Alan. It's only achievement that counts. That's why I want to make this Cape flight."

His shrewd eyes were examining her. "That'll mean more fame than ever."

She shrugged. "That's different." Before he could question her further she gave a shudder of anticipation. "Let's get the ballyhoo over as quickly as we can. Now I'm back in England I can't get home fast enough."

She looked like an excited child as she gazed at the broad river in the distance. "There it is. I always used to feel I was getting close to home when I saw the Humber."

Wright nodded. "We ought to be in Bridlington in the hour. Maybe less if we're lucky."

She sank back into the soft leather seat. Although a chilly wind was blowing outside, with the hood in position and the heater on, the limousine was warm and private. "Thank God that London ballyhoo is over. How did you think it went?"

"You were very good," he said. "Very professional."

She turned and stared at him. "Professional? You mean slick, don't you?"

"No, I wouldn't go that far."

"Yes, you would. I don't come from the North for nothing, Alan Wright. You think I've become a professional entertainer, don't you? Like the film stars who come over here. Well, don't you?"

His shrewd eyes twinkled. "Not yet. You still say the things you think, like on that broadcast last night. That's why people like you. But you've got to watch it."

"What does that mean?"

He shrugged. "Public entertainers have to please all the people all the time. You can't do that and stay honest. That's going to be your problem."

She knew now beyond any doubt why she needed this trip home. "Damn you, Alan, why are you always right?" Before he could make a self-deprecating comment, she went on: "Have you seen my parents since I left?"

"Yes, I've seen your dad. I hadn't heard from you for a long time, so I called round at his garage."

"I should have written more, I know. But I've been trying hard to get sponsors these last few months. How is dad?"

"He looked fine. He said your mum was well too. And that your sister was married and expecting a baby this year."

"Yes. Sometime in November, I think."

Wright nodded. "You know what's been puzzling me?"

"What?"

"The trouble you've had getting sponsors over there. After that Atlantic flight and all the publicity it brought you, you should have had sponsors queuing outside your door. Particularly in America."

Her hesitation was brief. She longed to share her innermost feelings with somebody and if there was one man in the world she could trust, she knew it was the sometimes sarcastic but always dependable Wright. She told him the story from beginning to end, omitting only any criticism, implied or otherwise, of McArthur's part in the affair.

With Wright making no comment until she finished, she had the feeling he was picking his questions carefully. "Did you both tell the press you'd shared the flight equally?"

"Yes. We said it on the radio too. But because I'm a woman the damned aviation experts automatically assumed he'd done all the difficult flying. Whereas, although Dean did wonders in the condition he was in, he couldn't be expected to stay awake for forty hours with the drugs he had to take."

Wright was silent for a moment. Then he shrugged. "I suppose in one way I shouldn't be surprised. I warned you in the beginning you'd be up against prejudice, didn't I?"

"Prejudice, yes. But this is something else. They won't accept the facts even when pushed right in front of their noses."

Wright opened his mouth to say something, then closed it again. Instead he grinned wryly. "You know your problem, don't you? You're too young and attractive. If you were plain and middle-aged they'd probably believe you."

Her indignation faded at his quip. "Are you saying I'll have to wait another ten or fifteen years to qualify?"

"No. You'd still be too pretty."

There was surprise as well as amusement in her laugh. "What's happened to you since I left? You never used to give a girl compliments like that. Have you got a girl-friend?"

"Me? Good Lord, no. As I said once before, crusty old bachelors like me don't get girl friends."

"That's nonsense. I think now I'm back I'll start looking around. You need a woman to go home to at nights."

Wright, as much in love with her as ever and secretly embarrassed by his compliments, scowled fiercely. "You'll mind your own business. At my age I'd get a dragon. Leave me to my little birds at Brook Lane. They're far less trouble."

Although she laughed, it was a comment that brought her ambition to the surface. "What's my Puss Moth like, Alan? I'm dying to see her."

"She's a beauty. Blue and silver. We haven't put extra fuel tanks in her yet: I felt you should decide what you want. But she's fully airworthy and ready for flight trials whenever you are."

"Who bought her?" she asked.

"The Old Man. After Paul told him what you wanted, of course."

"I suppose you haven't seen Paul for a long time?"

"No." Wright had noticed how her face lit up at his mention of Paul and knew the old flame was still alive. "How does he look these days?"

"Just the same. As young and handsome as ever."

Inwardly Wright winced. "Did you meet his wife?"

"No. But he's hoping to bring her over to England before my flight. So I might meet her then."

Wright nodded. "How's your husband?"

Without her intending it, her voice took on a defiant tone. "He's fine. You're wondering why he hasn't come over with me, aren't you?" When he did not answer, she went on: "I didn't want him to come. I want this to be my flight from the beginning to the end. Can you understand that?"

Wright hesitated, then gave a grimace. "After what's happened, yes, I think I can."

Her defiance fell away. "That's what I hoped. When can I see my plane? This afternoon?"

"Good Lord, no. Bridlington can't wait for you to arrive. You can't snub 'em all by staying out at Brook Lane. You can see it tomorrow."

Her face dropped. Close to home as she was, she had not taken into account the welcome the small town was sure to give her. "I must see mum and dad first. Can't we sneak in quietly along a back road?"

Wright gestured at the luxurious car. "In this thing?"

She pondered for a moment. "I've got it! Stop and we'll phone my dad. He can come out in one of his taxis and run me home. Afterwards he can bring me back to you and we can drive in as arranged. You don't mind waiting outside Brid for an hour or so, do you? I won't be any longer."

He was smiling at her ingenuity. "No, I don't mind. But what are we going to say when we arrive so late?"

"That's easy. We'll just say we've had a breakdown."

Wright nodded at the chauffeur who, with a glass partition between them, could hear nothing of their conversation. "You'll need to win him over!"

Her eyes twinkled at him. "I think I can do that. Don't you?"

"I've no doubt at all," Wright said with conviction.

Arthur Summers parked the old Austin taxi in the layby and eased his heavy body through the door. "Hello, lass. So you're home at last."

Delia threw her arms round his neck. "Hello, dad. It's good to see you again. Give me a kiss."

With typical Northern reserve, Arthur cast an embarrassed glance at Wright who was standing beside the limousine, before allowing the girl to plant kisses on his florid face. "You haven't been drinking, have you?"

She laughed. " 'Course I haven't. I'm just glad to see you, that's all."

"Aye. It's been a long time. But what's this performance for? Don't you know th' whole town's out in the streets waiting to welcome you?"

"I wanted to see you and mum first. What about Mary? Has she come?"

"Aye, she arrived with her husband yesterday. Why didn't you bring yours? Don't tell me you've broken up already?"

"Of course we haven't. I'll explain later. Can you get me home without being seen?"

"I dunno. They've gone mad back there. The phone's never stopped ringing this last week. Do you know they're giving you a big do in the Town Hall tonight?"

She nodded. "Yes. Alan's told me. You and mum are going, aren't you?"

" 'Course we are. Everybody's going. It's costing me the earth though. Mum's bought herself a new dress and made me get a suit. All to meet the bloody mayor."

She laughed and glanced at Wright, whose eyes were twinkling. "What about the garage?"

"You can't get workers any more. I took on a lad last month and all he thinks about is booze and girls. But we manage somehow."

"I'm sure you do. Shall we get along then? Alan's going to meet us here in ninety minutes. Is that all right?"

"Aye, I suppose so. But what about all them people? They'll think you've got lost."

She took his arm. "Another hour or so won't make any difference. Come on, dad. Let's go home."

THIRTEEN

The silver and blue high wing monoplane was standing like a poised bird in front of Brook Lane hangar. Delia's delight was infectious. "You're right, Alan. She's beautiful. When can I take her up?"

Wright glanced at the car-park at the side of the hangar. "If I were you, I'd wait until the Old Man arrives. He always likes to feel he's in charge. Was he at the presentation last night?"

She grimaced. "God, wasn't he just. You'd think he owned me from the way he acted. And I always thought our upper classes looked down their noses at publicity."

"That's just the image they project. In reality they don't miss a trick."

She laughed. "How does one take that? As a compliment or a criticism?"

He shrugged. "Take it any way you like."

Not for the first time she realized how little she knew about the private life of this diffident bachelor. "I think you're a socialist at heart. Am I right?"

"Aren't we all? Sometimes."

"Not all of us. My dad isn't. Or my mum. They'd touch their forelocks to Sir Richard any time of the day."

"What about you?" he asked.

"I don't know what I am. I suppose I've never thought much about politics. But I can't see myself curtseying to Sir Richard just because he's sponsoring my flight. I'm certain Paul had to make him see it was a good advertising gimmick before he took it on."

The arrival of the tycoon's car interrupted their conversation. Shooting stick at the ready, Sir Richard approached them. "My dear young lady! How are you this morning?"

"Better now," she told him. "But I'd a wicked hangover when I woke up."

From the way he was eyeing her, she felt he could have been assessing a new mare for his stables. "Yes, they gave you a handsome welcome, didn't they? And I understand they've got more lined up for you."

"Yes, but I shan't attend them all. I'm going to be too busy preparing for my flight."

He held up a hand. "Quite, quite, but I want you to consult me before you refuse any function. It might affect our plans." Before she could reply, he indicated the Puss Moth alongside them. "What do you thing of the aircraft we've bought you?"

It was easy to display enthusiasm for the sleek monoplane. "She's beautiful. I love her already."

"Yes, she's got good lines, hasn't she? And Wright says she's well built and lively. You haven't flown her yet, I take it?"

"No, Sir Richard. We were waiting for you."

Her reply clearly pleased him. "You can take her up later. First I want to talk about the plans we've made for you. You know that Mr Wright is going to be your general factotum?" When she nodded: "Are you happy with the arrangement?"

She smiled at Wright. "Yes, I am. Very happy."

"Good. I believe you said you'd like to be off in eight weeks time?"

"Yes. From all I'm told that should give the best overall weather conditions down to the Cape. As I'm crossing the equator I can't expect ideal conditions all the way, but at least it should avoid violent extremes."

Sir Richard nodded briskly. "That's our intelligence too. All right, young lady, let's go into the secretary's office and I'll show you what I've planned for you so far."

Back at home with her parents, Delia worked harder the next eight weeks than at any time in her life. Although she had the experience of the Atlantic flight behind her, she was soon reminded that a long-distance land crossing posed its own special problems. Landing rights in many countries that lay between England and the Cape had to be obtained, depots of oil and petrol had to be established, aircraft spares had to be purchased and distributed at strategic points. Although Wright shouldered most of the initial work, the perfectionist in her insisted she checked every detail herself.

In addition there were many refinements to be made to the Puss Moth which, in spite of its jaunty appearance, was only a standard factory model. Among these were the extra fuel tanks demanded by the flight. Every time one of these was installed, she had to carry out detailed tests to ensure flight stability was not lost. Endurance, altitude, and speed tests were a part of this programme, as well as the Moth's fuel economy at different heights in various weather conditions.

A further drain on her time were the functions Sir Richard insisted she attended, as well as her interviews with her other sponsors, in particular the *Daily Mail*, which was paying her handsomely for the exclusive rights in her flight. It meant she was seldom home until the late evening and even then she had not finished. There were logs to be filled in, notes of the next day's programme to be made, and one task she never forgot, her letters to McArthur.

Although she sometimes only managed a page or two, these letters were not a chore for her. She missed McArthur more than she had believed, particularly at nights when she crawled wearily into an empty bed. She poured her heart into the letters and also kept her word and phoned him twice a week.

In a way she regretted this promise. Although it was good to hear his voice, there were times when he sounded half-drunk and she could hear other voices, both male and female, in the background. Knowing his liking for women, she would wonder how long his promised chastity would last. Her jealousy would be fierce but in the end her common sense always came to the rescue. She had made the choice to leave him behind. She would have to accept the consequences to her marriage whatever they might be.

Yet she still missed him, and in more ways than personal ones. In spite of his competence as an engineer, Wright had no experience of long-distance flying. By leaving McArthur behind she had not only increased her burden but also reduced her chances of success.

Nevertheless she remained glad she had come alone. If she were successful, no one could take the credit from her again.

She also felt that McArthur's turbulent life-style and masterful behaviour would have been a distraction to her preparations.

Wright was very different, an undemanding person, always calm and always reliable. Moreover there was no sexual activity to complicate their relationship. After the turbulence of her last few weeks with McArthur, he was like an interlude in a violent symphony or a calm island in a stormy sea. More and more she found herself enjoying their few leisure hours together when they would sit chatting over a beer in the local pub or, as happened on two occasions, when they went to the movies together.

No two men could be more different, she sometimes thought, and yet she was prepared to take advice from either of them that she would not have welcomed from a younger man. She found this thought disturbing. Did it mean that basically she was a woman who needed a father figure?

It was a thought that brought more questions in its train. Sex, when practised as skilfully as McArthur practised it, could make a woman believe she was in love. Perhaps it was only when circumstances denied that sex to a woman that she was able to make a true assessment of her feelings.

Inevitably this thought chain would lead her to Paul. Because they had never had sex together, there had never been any physical beguilement to confuse her. So surely the fact that she felt the same way towards him when he was three thousand miles away as when they were sitting at the same table must be meaningful?

Nor did she feel any disparity of years with him, even although he too was older than she. Paul, handsome and exciting, was eternal youth and so in his case it could not be the little girl in her seeking emotional security.

For these reasons and more she convinced herself yet again as the weeks passed by that Paul was the great love of her life and one thought began to dominate her. When was he coming over to England?

Five more hectic days passed. She was working in the machine shop decarbonizing the Moth's Cirrus engine when Wright appeared in the doorway and motioned to her. Puzzled, she followed him outside the hangar, where he turned to her. "Sir Richard's just phoned. He say's Paul's due to dock on Friday."

She gave a start of excitement. "Friday? That's only three day's away."

He was watching her closely. "So?"

"The ship takes five days from America. Why hasn't Sir Richard told us before?"

"Why should he? I'm surprised he bothered to phone us now. It's hardly our business, is it?"

She gave a laugh. "Hardly our business!" Then she noticed his expression. "What are you looking at me like that for?"

He glanced round. Seeing a pilot and a pupil had walked out of the hangar, he took her arm and led her to one side of the tarmac. His voice was as blunt as she had ever known it. "Now you listen to me! Paul's married now. And so are you. So get rid of that torch you're carrying before it burns you. Do you understand me?"

She felt sudden anger. "What the hell are you talking about?"

"Don't play the innocent with me, girl. I've known you too long. Paul's in the net. And so are you. Remember that or you could get yourself into a pile of trouble."

Suddenly she was close to tears. "I don't know what you're talking about. Paul's just a good friend who's made this flight possible for me. So why shouldn't I be glad he's coming?"

"Glad he's coming is one thing. Acting as if you've a right to know his every move is something else."

"For heaven's sake, you're making a mountain out of a molehill."

His critical brown eyes seemed to be seeing right through her. "I don't think so. Personally I'm sorry he's coming at all. But as he is, remember one thing and keep on remembering it. You're here to break a record, not to break up a marriage."

The sound from the gramophone was deafening. Three couples, locked cheek to cheek, were slowly circling the living-room floor. Other couples in intimate postures were draped on settees and in armchairs. A few older men were standing round a table littered with liquor bottles and glasses. Outside the large, undraped windows a large moth was urgently tapping for entry into the overheated villa.

McArthur, tieless and in his shirt sleeves, was sprawled out on a settee. An attractive if dishevelled blonde, with the upper buttons of her dress unfastened, was sitting close to him. As the record ended and another one equally loud replaced it, she kicked off her shoes and tucked her silken, shapely legs beneath her. At the same time she snuggled closer and laid her head on McArthur's shoulder. "That's better, baby. Now someone should turn the lights out."

McArthur grinned. "You think John would like that?"

She raised her head and nodded at the table where an elderly man was exchanging jokes with his colleagues. "John wouldn't even notice, darling. He's past it. All he's interested in these days are his goddamned films."

"You should worry. He's made a star out of you, hasn't he?"

She grimaced. "What sort of star? All I am is a blown-up burlesque show girl."

"C'mon, baby. They love you out there. They think you've the best legs in the business."

"Yeah. That's the image he's given me. I want to be a real actress but you think the sonofabitch will give me a serious part? I do the flesh act and bring in the dough and he gives all his real parts to his blue-stocking girl friends."

He put a cigarette into her shapely mouth and lit it. "Why aren't people ever satisfied? There's a hundred million broads who'd give their eyeballs to be Judy Weldon."

She drew on her cigarette, then glanced at him quizzically. "Talking about being satisfied, how are you managing now that Delia's in Europe?"

He grinned. "I'm getting by."

"Who with?" When he did not answer, she went on: "The word's going around you've stayed on the straight and narrow since your marriage. Is that right?"

He exhaled smoke. "That's right. I've turned into a little boy scout."

"I don't believe you. Not now Delia's in Europe. Who's the lucky girl, honey?"

A smash of glass caught their attention. A drunken woman had reeled against the table and knocked a bottle of spirits to the floor. One of the men standing there kicked the broken glass under the table and the din and chatter returned. McArthur sat up. "How about another Bourbon?"

She drew him back. "Who're you sleeping with, Mac? Tell me."

"Nobody, honey. I'm taking a rest. They say it's good for a man."

"Don't you believe it. John took a rest three years ago and he's never woken up. How about you and me getting together again, baby? We're both lying in empty beds."

His heavy-lidded eyes moved over her. Somehow her *décolletage* had opened further and her dress was now halfway up her thighs. Feeling a familiar dryness in his throat, McArthur frowned. "Maybe some other time, honey. We're both too well known and this kid of mine doesn't know the rules."

"Then teach her the rules. You can't go out of circulation, Mac. It's not fair on us girls."

He shook his head. "It's not that easy. You know how the gossip magazines used to hound me in the old days. On top of them I've got Matt Hooper on my back."

She gave a giggle. "I think you're making excuses."

"I'm not making goddamned excuses. They've already mentioned my parties and that fight I had at Antonio's. Now Delia's not here, I've the feeling they're watching every move I make."

"So what? You're no different to the rest of us. That's the price you pay for being a celebrity." When he frowned again but did not answer, she went on: "Anyway, we're not going to do it in the street, honey. There are things like big limousines and secret places. Just give me a time and place and I'll be there."

McArthur wondered why he was hesitating. With all her faults, Judy was no tell-tale. As he gazed at her she pressed closer, her silken knees against his thighs, her scented hair against his cheek. "Remember how good I was to you last year, Mac? I'll be just as good again."

The blare of jazz died away. A woman flushed with drink staggered past McArthur to reach the records scattered round the foot of the gramophone. As McArthur drew back his outstretched legs to let her pass, he saw the outer door open. A moment later a brilliant flash gave a stark glimpse of the embracing couples sprawled round the room. Shouts and screams followed as a second photoflash went off. Half-blinded, with the girl still on his lap, McArthur saw three shadowy figures standing just inside the door. Cursing, he jumped to his feet. "You sons of bitches! Who said you could come in here?"

A third flash answered him. As he ran forward, one of the cameramen made the mistake of trying to pacify him. "It's O.K., Mac. We just wanted a few pictures. We're on our way now."

McArthur struck him full in the face. With a groan the man collapsed. About to attack the other two newsmen, McArthur had his arms grabbed from behind. "Steady, Mac! Take it easy, for Christ's sake."

It took four men to hold back the powerful and inflamed McArthur while the two startled newsmen dragged their colleague outside. As their car was heard driving away and McArthur was released, he swung round on the murmuring guests. "Who sent for those bastards? Who? I want to know."

The faces that stared back, all affected by drink, wore a variety of expressions. Some looked alarmed, others merely amused. No one answered McArthur although someone tittered. As he shouted at them again, the woman at the gramophone, too drunk to know what was happening, found the record she wanted and lowered the needle on it.

A blast of sound drowned McArthur's voice. Cursing again, he ran over to the gramophone and sent it crashing to the ground. Breathing hard, he swung round. "O.K., that's it! The party's over."

Muttering to one another, giving McArthur sullen looks, the guests began to leave. Judy's voice was malicious as she approached him. "Your skirt's showing, darling. Don't you want Delia to know the games you play when she's away?"

He moved as if to strike her. She drew back, then tut-tutted and blew him a kiss. "You'll never keep it up, you know. Chastity's not your strong point. I'll phone you in a couple of days."

Hips swaying, she crossed the room and took her husband's

arm. Five minutes later the room was empty. Left alone with the debris, McArthur poured himself a large Bourbon and dropped heavily into a chair.

FOURTEEN

The drizzle had ceased but the sky over Brook Lane was grey and threatening when the Puss Moth came into sight. As it banked over the hangar, two photographers began taking pictures. It made a complete circuit of the field, then, with engine throttled back, it flattened out and came in to land.

Moisture could be seen spraying from its wheels as it touched down. It ran a hundred yards or so, then, with engine blipping, it turned and began taxi-ing towards the hangar and the small party assembled before it.

Delia had noticed the visitors during her descent. At first she had paid them little attention: Sir Richard often allowed friends and business acquaintances to visit the airfield and meet her. It was only when the group was less than thirty yards from the Moth that she recognized the dark-haired, hatless man who, with a tall young woman beside him, was chatting to Wright as he watched the aircraft's approach.

The effect on Delia was electric, her heart suddenly racing as if injected by a potent drug. Almost without thinking she switched off the engine and began fumbling in her overall pockets for a comb. Peering through a side window, she saw Wright leading Paul and the young woman towards the aircraft. They were followed by the two cameramen.

She waited nervously for Wright to reach the Moth before she opened the door. Although her mouth was dry with nervousness, she managed a bright smile as she slipped down to the grass. "Hello, Paul. When did you get here?"

"Hello, Smudge." Leaning forward, he kissed her cheek before turning to the smiling girl at his side. "Darling, this is the famous flier you've heard so much about. Smudge, meet my wife, Gloria."

Delia found herself shaking the gloved hand of the American girl. It was a moment when her resentment spilled over as much on Paul as on Wright for picking such a time and place for the introduction. To be dishevelled and wearing oil-stained overalls against the American's elegant lamb's-wool coat was indignity enough. To be wearing flat shoes against the girl's high heels when the American was already a full three inches taller made her feel like a grubby urchin standing before a woman. Her lips felt stiff and her words sounded banal as she tried to smile. "Hello, Gloria. I'm pleased to meet you."

Although the American girl gave no indication of it, Delia felt certain she was aware of her discomfort. "Hello, Delia. Or should I call you Smudge?"

It took Delia all her time to smile. "I prefer Delia."

The American girl's poise and beauty made it easy for Delia to believe her amusement was condescending. "I don't blame you. But Paul has called you Smudge for so long, I've grown used to it. How are your preparations coming along?"

All Delia wanted at that moment was to escape. "All right so far." She glanced at Wright for help. "At least I think so."

Wright nodded. "Yes, we're on schedule. We should be ready for the eighth."

Delia was taking in more of the girl's appearance while Wright was speaking. The elegant black hat she was wearing not only matched her lamb's-wool coat but set off her thick, honey-coloured hair to perfection. With her height, she looked every inch a thoroughbred and Delia's stab of envy was painful.

Paul's question came as a relief. "How do you like the Moth? Is she behaving?"

"Oh yes, she's fine. She's coming through her trials well."

"Then you still have some more to do?"

"Yes. A few long-distance flights. To check her fuel consumption and my navigation."

He laughed. "Haven't you got it mastered yet?"

"I'm improving. But I could be a lot better."

Feeling Gloria's eyes assessing her in turn as she was speaking, Delia was relieved when one of the cameramen moved forward and said something to Paul. Nodding he turned to her. "The press would like a picture or two of us. You don't mind, do you?"

She glanced down at her overalls. "What? In these?"

"Why not? You look very professional."

She wanted to scream at him that she did not want to look professional: she wanted to look as chic and elegant as Gloria. "All right, if they must have them. Where shall we stand?"

The cameraman led Paul and herself to the front of the Moth. As the rest moved back, she glanced at Gloria. "Isn't she coming too?"

Paul shook his head. "This has something to do with the sponsorship." As she moved reluctantly closer to him, he gave her the smile that always turned her legs weak and put an arm round her waist. "We'd better look friendly, hadn't we, if it's going to be used for publicity purposes?"

She was afraid her embarrassment would be a give-away as they rejoined the rest of the party and she did not know how to take Gloria's invitation. "Paul and I are giving a small party next Friday. Why don't you come, Delia?"

For a moment she was tempted. At least she had the clothes to match the wealthy American: the contest would not be quite so one-sided. Then she noticed Wright's expression. "I'd love to but it might be difficult. There's so much to do before the eighth that we work most of the evenings."

"That's a shame. We'd both like to see you. Anyway, if you change your mind you can always give us a call."

Paul had opened the cockpit door and was examining the interior. Noticing him, Gloria gave her melodious laugh. "What is it, darling? Do you want to take her up?"

"What, and ruin Delia's chances by crashing her? It's a century since I flew. I'd need to take lessons these days."

In her eagerness Delia forgot herself. "Alan and I were taking her on a long load test tomorrow. Why don't you come in Alan's place?" Then, with embarrassment, she glanced at Gloria. "I'd take you both. But just to take one passenger we have to lighten her fuel load."

The American girl looked amused. "I shouldn't worry. I've promised to go with Paul's father to the races tomorrow. Paul isn't keen on horses and gambling, so I'm sure he'd love to go. Wouldn't you, darling?"

As Paul hesitated, Delia turned towards him eagerly. "Would you, Paul? Just this once. After all, it is your family's aircraft. You've got a right to use it."

Gloria answered for him. "He's just playing hard to get, Delia. You take him. Then I won't feel so guilty when I'm gambling."

"All right," Paul said. "It will be fun." He turned to Delia. "What time tomorrow?"

She was feeling breathless with excitement. "I was leaving around ten. Does that suit you?"

"Yes, ten's fine. Where are we going?"

"Up to Caithness and back. The mountains up there make it a bit more realistic."

Gloria glanced at her watch. "Now that's settled we'd better be on our way. We said we'd be home before five."

A minute later, followed by the cameramen and Wright, they made their way back to their car. As two mechanics took charge of the Moth, Delia started for the hangar. She was met at the entrance by Wright. His tone was hostile. "I suppose you're happy now?"

She tried to look innocent. "What does that mean?"

"You can't leave him alone, can you? Not even when his wife's with him."

The thought of flying with Paul again after that one magical day in her childhood had driven all other considerations from her. Now that she was reminded of them, her temper flared. "What's the matter with your mind these days? I've invited him for a flight in the aircraft his father's bought for me. Is that a crime?"

Although he did not answer her, his glance made her flush. "I don't have to take these insinuations from you, Alan. You do know that, don't you?"

The stocky, forthright Yorkshireman did not give an inch. "You'll get from me the things I believe. As you always have."

Her cheeks were pale with anger as she stared at him. Then she swung away and made for her car. "I'm going. I can't take any more of your damned sermons. Go to hell."

FIFTEEN

Delia suppressed a shiver as she climbed out of her car at Brook Lane on the following morning. It was still dark and a cold wind was sweeping across the field. Hurrying to the hangar side door to escape the cold, she was surprised to find it unlocked and lights shining over the Puss Moth standing inside.

The warm, welcome smell of a paraffin heater met her as she entered the machine shop. Wright, wearing oil-stained blue overalls, was standing before the stove, a mug in one hand and a sandwich in the other. He gave her a wry grin. "Cup of coffee?"

She was still feeling sullen with him after their quarrel the previous day. "I wouldn't mind."

He poured coffee from a flask into a mug. She eyed him warily. "Why are you here so early?"

He held out a small biscuit tin. "Sandwich?"

"No, thanks."

He handed her the mug. "I heard the weather forecast on the early news. There's a cold front of heavy cloud expected over Scotland later in the afternoon. In my opinion you ought to cancel your test."

Her face set. "I'm not cancelling it. There isn't the time left."

He gave a grimace of disgust. "There's time and you know it. But as Paul's going, I knew you wouldn't cancel. So I've been loading up your equipment. If you leave as soon as it's daylight, you should be back before the weather closes in."

"What about Paul?" she demanded.

"Give him a ring. If he wants the trip, he'll still come. Tell him you want to leave by eight o'clock. Eight-thirty at the latest."

She could not decide whether he was sincere or putting obstacles in her way. "Are you sure about that weather forecast?"

He nodded at the battered radio on the shelf. "Switch it on and hear it yourself." Draining his mug, he set it down on a bench. "I'm going to finish the job. No, drink your coffee first. There's not much left to do."

She sank down on a stool as he left the shop and pulled an envelope with an American postmark from her coat pocket. It had been given to her by her mother on her return home the previous evening. Knowing what it contained, she had not bothered to open it and had stuffed it into a pocket. Now, tearing open the flap, she pulled out a wad of newspaper cuttings and began paging idly through them.

One cutting was folded twice. Taking a sip of coffee, she opened it out, only to give a gasp of shock at the large photograph that stared up at her.

Her distress grew as she read the paragraph below the photograph. Showing a new interest in the cuttings, she began reading them in detail and was still reading them when Wright returned to the shop.

He noticed the change in her immediately. "What's the trouble?"

"Nothing," she said defensively.

He drew nearer. "Those are press cuttings, aren't they?"

She gave a defiant nod as she began pushing them back into the envelope. "Yes. I took out a year's subscription five months ago."

"What for?"

"If the American press changed their minds about me, I wanted to know."

"Change their minds in what way?"

"About the part I played in the flight. It was important to my chances of getting sponsorship."

He understood now but was puzzled by her distress. "Have they changed their minds?"

"One or two have. But no more."

He held out his hand. "Can I look?"

She pushed the envelope back into her coat pocket. "Some other time. Let's get this job finished first."

"It is finished. You can take off as soon as you like."

It was the diversion she was looking for. "Then I'll phone Paul. Did you say eight-thirty?"

"Eight o'clock's better. I don't want you taking chances at this stage in the game."

She met his eyes defiantly. "Eight-thirty. I'll go and phone him."

His voice checked her as she was crossing the shop. "You'll have to phone from the secretary's office. I haven't switched over the extension yet."

She was grateful for the chance to escape. She paused at the door. "Thanks for coming in so early, Alan. I appreciate it."

She could feel his eyes following her as she turned and made for the office. She hoped the sob that broke from her did not reach him.

The Puss Moth lurched as the couple changed places. Dropping back into the pilot's seat, Delia steadied the aircraft, then glanced at Paul who was fastening his safetly belt. "I've told you. It's like swimming or cycling: you never forget how to do it."

He laughed. "Smudge, don't be kind to me. I was over-correcting all the time."

"That's only because she's heavily loaded. Did you enjoy it?"

"Of course I did."

"Then why don't you take up flying again? America's a marvellous place for it."

"Perhaps I will. We'll see."

They were returning from Caithness. As Wright had warned, the weather had been deteriorating for the last hour and the cloud base was now down to two thousand feet. Inwardly Delia was hoping it would not deteriorate further. With her record attempt only a week away, she was becoming hypersensitive to any threat, however slight, that might cause its postponement or cancellation.

At the same time she felt the danger was slight. They were flying with the weather, they were less than ninety minutes from Brook Lane, and she still had two thousand feet of clear air space for her navigation. With any luck at all they would be home well before the weather closed right in.

Below, wisps of cloud kept glazing the autumn fields. With Paul safely back in his seat, she took the Puss Moth down another couple of hundred feet. To her left the gun-metal sea could hardly be distinguished from the clouds that mantled it.

She glanced at Paul. "How does Gloria like England?"

"She loves it. She always has, particularly London. After we've seen you off next week, I've promised to take her to some of the shows."

"How long will you stay over here?"

He looked surprised by her question. "Until you get back, of course. We can't miss the celebrations, can we?"

Suddenly she felt nervous. "Do you think I can do it, Paul?"

"I'm sure you can. I've never doubted it."

She had never loved him more. "I'm going to do my best. You can rely on that."

Before he could reply, there was a loud splintering crack and thick red fluid splattered across the windshield. Another crack sounded a second later and the Moth gave a violent lurch. At the same moment the steady roar of its engine rose into a high- pitched scream.

Shouting at Delia, Paul tried to reach the throttle. Recovering, fighting to prevent the Moth spinning, Delia reached out and jerked the throttle back.

The scream died but the engine note held a loud slapping sound and the Moth was still trying to spin. Delia turned her startled face to Paul. "What happened?"

He pointed at the blood-stained windshield. "We must have hit a large bird. Switch right off."

She realized he was right: a blade of the propeller must have splintered away, causing the uneven torque. She switched off and immediately the Moth's stability returned and the slapping sound was replaced by the whine of airfoils.

As they searched the countryside below for a place to land, Paul pointed at a large grassy field near the coast that was surrounded by stone hedges. "That looks promising. What do you think?"

She nodded and banked towards it. "You don't want to take over, do you?"

He grimaced and shook his head. "Good heavens, no.

You're the skipper."

She thought how similar the situation was to her forced landing in America. Yet one thing was dissimilar: her fear. Then it had been of death or injury. Now it was the threat to her record attempt. That it should take precedence over the danger to herself or to Paul gave her another insight into the depth of her ambition.

In her anxiety not to damage the Moth, she found herself too stiff on the controls and tried to relax. "Which way's the wind blowing down there? Can you tell?"

Paul pointed at the rain now slanting down. "I think it's still blowing from the land. But I can't be sure."

She gingerly guided the Moth down and at 800 feet banked over the sea. Below the high Northumberland cliffs reeled and steadied. She tried to sound calm. "How am I doing?"

He lifted a thumb and smiled. He looked very calm, she thought, but she had expected that of Paul. The irony of the situation did not escape her. Since first learning to fly she had longed to demonstrate her prowess to him and been denied the chance. Now it had come with a vengeance.

The Moth glided over one stone hedge and then another. A flock of sheep lifted their heads, stared aghast at the approaching plane, then turned and fled.

Delia was low enough now to see thick clumps of grass and molehills. For one heart-stopping moment she feared the Moth's descent would not stretch to the third hedge and she was rigid in her seat as it slid towards her. As it disappeared below she held her breath but there was no impact and a second later the Moth was shuddering and bouncing over the uneven field. As she fought to hold it steady, she heard Paul's voice. "Well done!"

The Moth came to a halt in the middle of the large field. With its power gone, she knew it would have to remain there. As she sat recovering, she heard for the first time the moan of the wind and the rattle of rain on the aircraft's taut fabric.

"Are you all right?" Paul asked.

She pulled herself together. "I am now. I was afraid I might damage her."

"The propeller must have been flawed to splinter that way. You brought her down quite beautifully."

She could have listened to his praise for the rest of the afternoon but made herself stir. "Did you notice any houses nearby?"

"No. But there's a road a couple of fields away. I'll go and look for a phone."

She gazed across the desolate scene and thought about his leg. "No, it's better I go. I've more chance of getting a lift than a man has. You stay and look after the plane."

His voice turned impatient. "Nonsense. We might be miles from a telephone." Then, as he followed her gaze across the rain-swept fields: "On second thoughts we'd both better go. It'll be dark soon and I can't leave you here alone."

"No," she said sharply. "I'm not leaving the plane unguarded."

"Why not? Who's going to harm it?"

"No," she said again. "I'm not risking having it vandalized the way our Bellanca was. Besides, there's all my equipment on board. I'm going to stay with her."

"You mean the whole night?"

"Why not?" She indicated the packed cabin behind her. "I've got all my survival equipment with me, a tent, blankets, a pressure stove, even food." His expression made her smile. "Come to think of it, it could be a useful exercise."

He sighed. "If anyone has to stay with her then I will. But we'll talk about it when I get back."

She dragged an oilskin from behind her seat and before he could stop her, threw open the cabin door and jumped down. "Put the tent up while I'm away, will you?"

He made a last effort to change her mind. "Nobody's going to vandalize her here, Smudge. Let's go together and come back at first light."

She was already on her way across the drenched field. "I'll be back as soon as I can," she shouted. "Make yourself a cup of coffee in the meantime."

SIXTEEN

It was over an hour before she returned. The light had almost gone and the Moth was only a dark silhouette across the field. The heavy rain had ceased but there was still a fine drizzle in the wind.

At first she could not see the tent but as she neared the Moth she saw a faint phosphorescent glimmer at its far side. Rounding the aircraft she saw the light came from the small ridge tent that Paul had set up. Squatting down, she peered inside. "I'm back. Is everything all right?"

He was sitting on a blanket that was spread over the ground sheet. Alongside him was a small pressure stove with a simmering kettle standing on it. He looked relieved at seeing her. "Did you find a phone?"

She removed her oilskin and shoes and then crawled inside, conscious of her wet, bedraggled hair. "Yes, although I'd trouble getting a lift. There weren't many cars and in my oilskin and overalls I suppose people thought I was a man. The phone was a good three miles away, in a layby."

"Did you get Wright?"

"After a bit of a struggle, yes. By the way, I asked him to phone your home and tell them what's happened."

He nodded. "Thanks. So what about the propeller?"

"Our spare hasn't arrived yet, so Alan can't drive up with it tonight. He said he'd phone de Havilland's right away but he's sure they won't fly one up to him before the morning. Once it arrives he'll bring it himself."

He nodded at the tent entrance. "Even if we had one we couldn't fly out of here tonight." His eyes moved to her wet overalls. "I still think you should find somewhere to stay tonight. You need a hot bath and a change of clothes."

97

"I'll be all right. I've got dry things in the Moth. But what about you? Perhaps I should have asked Alan to come right away. At least he could have found you accommodation for the night."

He shook his head. "No, it's better he waits for the propeller. In any case, he probably wouldn't find us in the dark. And if he did, we couldn't leave you here alone."

"Why not? I won't have company in Africa if I have to make an emergency landing."

He frowned. "Let's hope that won't happen."

She nodded and wriggled to the tent entrance. "I'll go and change now. Then we'll have something to eat." She returned ten minutes later, wearing clean overalls, fresh make-up, and with her wet hair combed and tidy. "That's better. I feel human again." Crawling in, she laid a flask on the blanket. "Brandy," she told him. "Part of my emergency rations."

His eyes rolled comically. "Luxury indeed."

She noticed that a pan had taken the place of the kettle and leaned over it. "What's in there?"

"More of your rations. Corned beef and vegetables."

Dry and clean again, pleased at her performance in landing the Moth safely, she was now feeling almost euphoric at being alone in his company. In the dim light of the stove her eyes shone at him. "I didn't know you could cook too."

His shapely mouth quirked. "Cometh the hour, cometh the man!" He handed her a mug of coffee. "Here, drink this. It'll warm you up."

"What about you?" she asked, knowing there was only one mug.

"That's all right. I've had mine."

They ate half an hour later. Afterwards a silence fell between them and she knew what it signified. Feeling it had to be said again even though it went against her desires, she poured brandy into the mug and handed it to him. "You could still get a lift to the nearest village if you went soon, you know. Why don't you?"

At that moment the stove hissed and went out, leaving them in semi-darkness. She laid a hand on his arm as he stirred. "I wouldn't bother. The paraffin might be difficult to find in the dark. Unless you want another coffee later, that is."

He sank back and took a sip of brandy. She gazed at him. "Did you hear what I said?"

"Yes, I heard. But I'm not leaving you alone. I can go and sleep in the Moth later on."

She sank back in relief. An hour passed while they sipped in turn at the brandy. Outside the rain had stopped but the wind was plucking at the thin canvas. He passed over a sleeping-bag. "It's going to be a cold night. Cover yourself with this."

"What about you?"

"I didn't get wet. In any case I'm going to look for that paraffin. The stove helps to keep the tent warm."

He returned fifteen minutes later. "I can't find any. Are you sure you put some in?"

"No. Perhaps Alan forgot." She unzipped the sleeping-bag. "Put this over you. I don't want it all."

He hesitated, then obeyed. With the stove no longer between them, his arm was only inches from her own and once again she could feel her skin burning as if they were in contact. She wondered if he felt the same. As she willed him to move closer, she felt full of guilt and weak with anticipation.

They spoke little in the hour that followed. Once she believed he had fallen asleep until he quietly opened the tent flap and gazed out.

"What is it?" she asked.

He turned to her. "I thought you were asleep. It looks as if that front is passing over. The clouds are breaking."

She saw he was right. A watery moon was waxing and dimming. She sank back on the blanket. "I've just remembered something. I forgot to ask Alan to phone my mum and dad."

"He won't forget. Alan's thoughtful about things like that."

She knew he was right. They smoked a cigarette and then finished the brandy. She felt light-headed as she lay back and knew she had drunk too much. "Paul."

"Yes?"

"How is Gloria going to take this?"

She felt him start. "What do you mean?"

"You know. Just the two of us here?"

For a moment he sounded hostile. "She won't think anything. Why should she?"

"No. Of course not. I'm sorry, Paul."

There was a tension between them that had not been there before. He tossed the stub of his cigarette out on the wet grass, then turned towards her. "What about Dean? Will he make a fuss?"

Her dormant anger stirred. "He's no right to make a fuss about anything. Not after the way he's been behaving."

There was enough light in the tent now for her to see his enquiring eyes but he did not speak. She knew it was the brandy that was making her talk but she was powerless to stop. "I had some Press cuttings yesterday. Most of them were from those awful gossip magazines they have in the States. There was also a photograph. I thought Dean had changed since we met but it seems he hasn't. I suppose it was too much to expect."

He was silent for a moment, then he said quietly. "I'm sorry, Smudge. I thought you were happy."

Suddenly her eyes were wet with tears. "So did I. I realize now I shouldn't have left him behind. Only I felt I had to do this flight by myself."

"You are sure about this? You mustn't believe everything you read in those magazines, you know. Most of the time they exaggerate or tell a pack of lies."

"There was a photograph, Paul. They couldn't invent that." Suddenly the dam that was holding back her inhibitions and longings collapsed and she threw herself into his arms. "Oh, Paul, why wasn't it you and me? We'd have been so happy. I know we would."

He tried to draw back but she clung to him more tightly. "I love you so much. I've loved you ever since that day we first met."

He tried to handle it lightly. "You were only a little girl then, Smudge."

"I don't care what I was. I haven't changed towards you. I'll never change." Her grip tightened. "Make love to me, Paul! Just this once. Please."

His face was troubled as he gazed down at her. "We've both had a lot to drink, Smudge. Let's not do anything we might regret."

"I won't have any regrets. Never."

"You can't be sure of that," he said quietly. "But in any case, I might. Have you thought about that?"

His words seemed to stun her for a moment. Then she shivered and her tear-stained face lifted. "I haven't thought about you at all, have I? My God, I'm selfish, Paul. I'm the most selfish bitch in the world."

His hand ran over her hot forehead and down her wet cheek. "No. You're just a little drunk, that's all. As I am. Why don't you think about that record you're going to break next week and try to get some sleep."

She pressed closer to him. "The flight you've made possible. That's the thing I love about it most of all. If I do go to sleep, will you stay here with me? You won't go and sleep in the Moth?"

He smiled. "I'll stay. If you promise to be good."

Her head snuggled into his shoulder. "I'll be good. Just don't go away, that's all. It's so good to be close to you like this."

He soothed her and her eyes closed. It was all right, she told herself. Paul loved her, so much so that he wanted to do nothing that might harm her future. He was wrong about that, as men so often are wrong, but that did not matter. He loved her more than his own self-gratification. Only Paul could love that way.

She was less sure about herself. A moment ago she had wanted sex with him like a parched man craving water. Yet now that craving had turned into a contentment that was soaking into her like melted butter. Fuddled by the brandy, she put it down to her forced landing which required a gentler kind of comfort from him.

It would all come right one day, she told herself. Somehow, sometime, it would all come right because they both loved one another and their kind of love could not be denied for ever. It was her last warm and comforting thought before she fell asleep like an innocent child in his arms.

She took off from Croydon at exactly ten a.m. the following Wednesday. The dense crowd of reporters, well-wishers and friends packing the airport gave a great cheer as her tiny Puss Moth began to roll forward along the runway. Car hooters blared out and Union Jacks waved as the plane began to pick up speed.

The cheers died as the heavily-loaded Moth rose a few feet and then fell back. Among the knowledgeable in the crowd, lungs became tight and nails bit into palms when the Moth had covered half the length of the runway and still failed to respond. When at last it sluggishly rose and cleared the distant houses, a cheer followed it that could be heard right across Croydon.

Two circling aircraft fell into formation behind the Moth to escort it to the coast. As they too crossed the airfield perimeter, cameramen began packing away their tripods, men lit cigarettes, and in a buzz of conversation the crowd began to disperse.

Only two men stood watching until the tiny speck that was the Moth finally vanished into a low bank of cloud. Paul's attention was broken by Gloria touching his arm. Wright needed a word from his chief mechanic before turning and walking back to his car.

SEVENTEEN

McArthur pushed open the front door, caught her in his arms, and carried her into the living-room. "Welcome home, honey."

She gave a gasp of pleasure. The large room was full of flowers of every description. "Don't tell me these are all from you?"

His grin was almost sheepish. "It's just a way of saying I'm glad to see you home."

As he put her down she kissed him. "You didn't have to go this far. They must have cost you a fortune."

"You're worth a fortune, honey."

She gave him a look, then moved round the room examining the blooms. "They're set out so beautifully too. Who did that? The florist?"

He followed her, clearly delighted by her reaction. "With a bit of help from friends and Mrs Levinsky."

Mrs Levinsky was the housekeeper she had found for him before her departure, a woman as English as fish and chips in spite of her improbable name. Which of his friends he referred to she did not ask. Her decision not to confront him with the photograph and the snippets of gossip had been made during her flight to and from the Cape. During long and lonely hours in the air, when death or serious injury had been her constant companions, she had found herself facing her own conscience. She had known before marriage the kind of man he was and yet she had left him behind, in spite of his entreaties, to pursue her own ambition. Was he then entirely to blame for what had happened?

Nor could she forget her behaviour with Paul. Selfrighteousness argued she would not have asked him to make love to her if she had not received the tell-tale photograph from America but she did not believe it. She had been as unfaithful in her mind with Paul as Dean had been with his girl friends. She had even married him knowing she was in love with Paul. The only difference in their behaviour had been opportunity. She had only one marriage. On her return home she would forget the past and live as if nothing had happened.

Up to the present she had not found it difficult. McArthur's welcome in New York could not have been more loving and her own pleasure at seeing him again had surprised her. Their love-making that night had been as passionate and uninhibited as on the first day of their marriage.

McArthur had paused by the cocktail cabinet. "How about a drink, honey? To celebrate your homecoming."

"Just a little one," she said. "Did you say there's a lot of mail for me?"

He nodded at her dressing-room. "Yeah. Sackfuls. It started coming in even before you docked." He waved her back. "Don't look at it now, for Christ's sake, or I won't see you for the rest of the week."

She sank down on the settee while he poured the drinks. Noticing the size of the whisky he was giving himself, she took in his appearance again. There was no doubt that his eyes were more pouched and the skin of his cheeks slacker than before she left for England. "I hope you haven't been doing too much drinking while I've been away."

He grinned over his shoulder. "You kidding? I've hardly touched the stuff."

"I'll bet," she said.

He brought the drinks over and set them on a small table by the settee. Then he took her in his arms. "It's good to have you to myself again, baby. You can't imagine."

She returned his kiss, then laughed and pushed him away. "You make it sound as if I'd just got back."

"You've just got back home, honey. That's different to hotel rooms, railroad cars, and the ballyhoo."

"But you've always liked the ballyhoo. You're the big playboy, remember?"

"Yeah, but that's something else. I've missed my girl and it's great to have her back home with me."

It was eight days since she had arrived in New York to the hooting of sirens and the fountains of water from tugs and lighters. Flags and bunting had fluttered from ships and buildings, thousands of cheering well-wishers had lined the quays. No royal personage had received a greater welcome from New York than Delia that day.

McArthur had been the first on board and they had spent fifteen minutes in her cabin before going out together to face the jostling mob of reporters. In spite of her resolutions she had expected to feel some reserve at their first meeting but what little there was had disappeared the moment he took her in his arms. For his part he had shown nothing but effusiveness and would have made love to her there and then but for her protests and the impatient crowd waiting outside.

Only one thing had marred the day. McArthur had clearly been drinking freely beforehand and it had shown in small but revealing ways when they went out to meet the jostling reporters. Knowing by this time how the Press scrutinized every act, no matter how tiny, of their self-made idols, she was afraid of the conclusions that might be drawn from his condition.

To be fair to him, however, he had kept relatively sober during the days that followed. If anything New York's welcome had eclipsed the one given her and McArthur after their Atlantic flight and at times it had seemed that everyone who was anyone in America had wanted to shake hands or kiss the girl who had flown alone to Cape Town and back and broken every record set by men.

With the limelight now hers alone, it had been McArthur's habit to take her to a function, remain with her until the initial fanfares were over, and then unobtrusively disappear. Afterwards she had usually found him in some quiet corner, drinking with a few close friends.

If occasionally she had felt embarrassed that he was having to take a back seat to her, it was embarrassment easy to disperse. Dean had enjoyed his full share of stardom and on the last occasion had owed his fame to her. She had no cause to feel discomfort in her present role: it had been doubly earned. And Dean's turn would come again.

He was lifting his glass to her. "To you, honey. To a terrific performance but most of all to having you home again."

She felt very warm towards him at that moment. "Thanks Dean. It's very good to be home again."

"I didn't miss a news bulletin during your flight. But I think the worst part was waiting for you after you got back. I'd forgotten they'd want to wine and dine you over there. Those three weeks were the longest of all."

It ought to have been three months to avoid hurt feelings, she was thinking. Two hundred thousand people had been waiting at Croydon Airport for her arrival, light aircraft had buzzed their salutes, searchlights had lit up the sky. The nine-mile route through London to her hotel had been lined with people five and six deep. It had been a night neither she nor London would ever forget.

Honours had fallen on her like confetti in the days that followed. The *Daily Mail* had presented her with a gold cup and a cheque for twelve thousand pounds. She had been enrolled into the Guild of Air Pilots and Navigators of the British Empire and made an honorary member of the Society of Engineers. Invitations had poured in from all sides. On the sixth day had come the greatest honour of all: an invitation to Buckingham Palace where she had been invested with the C.B.E. by the smiling King Emperor.

Not all had been sweetness and light, however. Rumours that civic dignitaries in her home town were becoming disgruntled by her delay in visiting them had forced her and her parents to make a hasty dash up north. She had done her best at the subsequent banquet to smooth ruffled feathers but she was no more of a diplomat than the rest of her fellow Yorkshiremen and the evening had not been a success.

The truth was she had been desperately tired. The record-breaking double flight had been a great strain mentally and physically – throughout it she had never enjoyed more than three hours sleep a night – and she had badly needed rest.

Instead the *Daily Mail* had wanted her to tour the country giving lectures. As the newspaper had been one of her principal sponsors it was not an unreasonable request but she could not face it. Instead she had pointed out that she had not seen her husband for over four months and asked if they would postpone the tour until she returned. Somewhat frigidly, the

Mail had granted her request.

On one score she was greatly relieved. Knowing Sir Richard was also not above demanding his pound of flesh, she had half-expected he would want to use her for marketing purposes. When he did not, she felt certain Paul had spoken for her.

Along with Sir Richard and Wright, Paul and Gloria had been the first to welcome her back to Croydon but the couple had left for America a few days later. Before following them, she had made a special journey up to Brook Lane. With enough money now to afford a full-time engineer, she had asked Alan Wright if he would go with her. "I need a manager and an adviser too, Alan. You did a terrific job for me on the Cape flight. Will you come? Please!"

He had given her his wry grin. "You've got a husband to manage you, girl. You don't need me. Besides, I've got a job here. It'll do until my pension."

"I need you in other ways, Alan. You're a fellow Yorkshireman. You're good for me."

"You mean I keep you on the straight and narrow and don't let you get big-headed? Aye, that's true. But I wouldn't fit in over there. You know I wouldn't."

She knew he was right but had felt a sense of loss on saying goodbye to him. After a last visit to her parents she had returned to London and two days later boarded a ship for New York.

Her feelings had been mixed when she waved goodbye to the large crowd that had gathered to say farewell. There had been sadness at leaving her country and her friends; there had been anticipation at seeing Dean again; and there had been a deep, inner satisfaction. Although it had taken her two dangerous ventures, she now felt justified in believing that she was at last accepted on both sides of the Atlantic as a first-class pilot in her own right, the relatively modest ambition she had set herself after her first flight with Paul a decade ago.

McArthur had finished his whisky and was eyeing her glass. "Those Limeys have slowed you down, baby. Drink up and have another."

"No. I'm going to have a bath and change. What about dinner tonight? Do you want to go out?"

"Go out? We've just got home, baby."

"I know but unless Mrs Levinsky's been shopping, I'll have nothing to give you."

"Mrs Levinsky has been shopping but that's not what we're having tonight. Dinner's being brought round at eight, with wine and champagne to match. O.K.?"

"When did you order that?"

"I left instructions with Mrs Levinsky. It's O.K. She's reliable."

She laughed and threw her arms round his neck. "You can be very sweet, Dean. I think I'd forgotten that."

"You know something?" he said, reaching out for her in the darkness. "I got jealous when you were over there."

She thought he was talking about Paul. "When, darling?"

"Every day. All I seemed to see in the papers were photographs of you with some new guy. Commissioners, Governor-Generals – you seemed to be meeting every important guy in Africa."

She pressed against him. "I was a novelty – a girl dropping out of the sky in a tiny aeroplane. It broke the monotony for them."

His hand ruffled her hair. "Yeah, I can believe that. Who was that good-looking guy you met in Cape Town? I must have seen half a dozen photographs of you and him together."

"Oh, he was a colonel in their army. A kind of bodyguard-cum-adviser-cum-escort." With her naked body pressed against his own, she felt safe to tease him. "He was good-looking, wasn't he?"

"Too goddamn good-looking. Don't go to the Cape again, honey."

She laughed. "No. It's going to be Australia the next time."

There was a sudden silence. Then he stirred. "Australia?"

"Sir Richard, Lord Wakefield, and the other sponsors would like me to try for the light plane record. They think I've every chance of getting it." Then she remembered. "It needn't affect our dual flight, Dean. We can do that first if you want."

He reached for a cigarette. As a match flared, she caught sight of his bearded face. He dropped back on his pillow and the cigarette glowed before he spoke again. "What about the other thing?"

"What other thing?"

"The thing marriages are supposed to be for. Babies."

"Oh, that. There's no hurry about that, is there? I'm still young."

"You're still young, baby, but what about me?"

She laughed. "It doesn't matter how old a man is, does it? The way you are, you'll probably be able to father babies when you're eighty."

"I don't want babies when I'm eighty, honey. I want them while I'm still young enough to enjoy them."

She bit her lip. "Dean, you don't want to saddle me with babies just when I've achieved my ambition and made a name for myself, do you?"

"Wasn't that what we agreed?"

"I don't think so. Not right away. Otherwise how were we to make that dual flight together?"

He went silent again, his cigarette glowing and fading in the darkness. Desperately wanting to avoid a quarrel with him on her first day home, she laid her head against his shoulder. "Dean, I'm tired. We're both tired. Can't we talk about this some other time?"

He stirred as if his thoughts had been far away. "Yeah, O.K. We'll talk later."

They made love shortly afterwards but it was not the same. Although her body reacted with its usual enthusiasm, her mind was less committed and she knew why. It was not only the resentment both were feeling: it was also lack of trust. On her part, relying on him until now to provide contraception, she had been able to respond with spontaneity to his love-making. Now, conscious he felt he was being cheated, she would have to take her own precautions. With both spontaneity and trust gone, their love-making could never be the same again. It was a thought that both inhibited and depressed her.

EIGHTEEN

The Press cuttings with Delia's triumphant arrival in New York arrived two days later. Afraid what they might contain, she had hoped to collect them from the post box before McArthur awoke but he was up early that morning and caught sight of her walking back up the drive with the thick envelope in her hand.

He met her at the door. "What is it, baby? You keen to read all the good things they say about you?"

She smiled. "Yes, why not?"

To her dismay he took the packet from her. "I guess I'm as keen as you are. Let's take a look."

She followed him helplessly into the living-room while he tore open the envelope. Dropping into a chair she watched his face as he began reading the cuttings. Her heart sank as his look of pleasure turned into a frown. "What's the matter?" she asked.

Ignoring her he continued reading the slips of newsprint. Inwardly tense, she lit a cigarette. As she exhaled smoke, she heard him curse. Rising, she went to his side. "What is it, darling?"

He thrust a cutting at her. "The sonofabitch! Take a look at that."

His photograph stared back at her. Below it was the caption: DEAN MCARTHUR CELEBRATES DELIA'S HOMECOMING. Her eyes ran down the paragraph that followed. 'Mac was in mellow form when his beautiful wife made her triumphant return to New York yesterday. After offering an empty hip flask to the army of newsmen, he pretended to be one of them by borrowing a pencil and pad and interrogating her himself. He completed his comic act by taking a flag from one of her admirers and fastening it in the buttonhole of his overcoat.

'It was noticeable, however, that in the subsequent receptions given to Delia, he was far less conspicuous. Was he playing the gallant gentleman and making certain this time that he took no credit from his plucky young wife or did his absence mean he has realized that while her star has risen high into the firmament of fame, his has sunk into a Bacchanal of wild parties and forgotten dreams?'

Her eyes lifted. "Who wrote this?"

"Hooper's behind it," he said. "Who else?"

She read the title on the cutting. "This isn't the *Los Angeles Times*. It's one of those gossip magazines. In any case, it's not Hooper's style."

"He doesn't write the stuff himself. He gives his copy to a sob sister who cuts him in on the fee."

"Are you sure about this?"

"It's what I was told by a newshawk. He said most of them do it."

She was paging through the rest of the cuttings. "Here's the one from the *Los Angeles Times*. It doesn't have any snide reference to you. Here, read it!"

He pushed the cutting away. "He wouldn't say it in the *Times*. He crawls in the back way." He swung round. "I'm going to see the sonofabitch."

"No," she said sharply. "That would only make things worse."

"So what am I supposed to do? Sit and take it?"

"Just forget it. Nobody takes any notice of these gossip magazines."

"That proves you're still a kid, baby. It's dirt people want to believe."

"Come on, Dean. Nobody believes you're finished. That's ridiculous."

His mood suddenly changed. "I wish I was so goddamned sure, baby. I wish we were both so sure."

Caught by surprise, she stared at him. "What does that mean?"

His laugh was bitter. "Come on, baby. Don't tell me you haven't any doubts either."

"I haven't," she lied, "but that doesn't help you. Why don't you fight back and make fools of them? Announce you're going to make another solo flight. You should still be able to get sponsors. Only you must do it soon."

"Why's that, baby? I thought nobody thought I was on the slide."

She saw that only honesty could save him. "It's no secret you've been drinking a lot recently. That's why people are talking this way. So prove them wrong. Hit the headlines and make me proud of you."

His bitterness was not so easily eroded. "And forget about the dual flight and the baby? Right, kid?"

She bit back her sharp reply. "A dual flight won't help you now – not after this Cape flight of mine. You have to do a solo yourself, the way I had to." Her voice softened as she read his expression. "Show them all how wrong they are, Dean. Do it for me."

He lit a cigarette and sucked in smoke. Seeing how his hands were trembling, she suddenly began questioning the wisdom of her pleas. She watched him take a few paces across the room and pick up an ornament from a shelf. As he toyed with it, she could almost feel him bracing himself. After a few seconds, he turned, "I guess you're right, honey. It is the only way to answer them. O.K. I'll do it."

"Yes, but are you sure you want to?" she asked.

"Yeah, I am. I should have done it before." He paused, then gave her a grin. "Let's make it a big one. L.A. to Alaska."

"Do you think that's wise? Wouldn't L.A. to New York be better?"

He paused outside his room door. "No, damn it. In for a penny, in for a pound, as you're always saying."

He returned a minute later wearing a coat. "Where are you going?" she asked.

He grinned and kissed her. "Into town, honey. I'm going to tell 'em all first hand. The sooner it gets in the press and on radio, the sooner it'll bring in the sponsors."

Full of apprehension now, she wanted to talk to him further before the die was cast. But seeing his expression as he left the villa she knew it was too late.

The cars were parked on both sides of the road before and beyond the villa. Delia, who had spent the afternoon shopping in Los Angeles with a friend, felt both surprise and gratification as she drove past them. McArthur's star, she felt, could not have fallen that far if his previous day's announcement had brought such a media response.

It was an illusion that was brutally shattered when she turned into the drive. Reporters, who had moved aside to allow her car through, closed around her like an engulfing tide when she stepped out. At first she could make no sense of their questions.

"Where've you been, Delia? To see Hooper?"

"Hey, Delia. Give us the lowdown. Who's telling the truth?"

"What are your comments on the *Times* article, Delia?"

Bewildered by the onslaught, she fought her way to the villa. "I don't know what you're all talking about. Let me through, please."

Dishevelled, confused, with one parcel lost and trampled underfoot, she reached the front door. It was opened by Mrs Levinsky whose formidable presence halted the baying mob. A shrill feminine voice, reaching Delia before Mrs Levinsky could close and bolt the door, brought her a chilling hint of what was behind the outcry. "Who's telling lies, Delia? You or Matt Hooper?"

With newshawks prowling round the villa and peering through windows, McArthur had taken refuge in the library. The blinds were half-closed, subduing the sunlight outside. As she entered, she saw him sitting at the desk with his back to her, a half-empty whisky bottle on the floor beside him. "For God's sake, what's going on out there, Dean? What's happened?"

For a moment he did not move. Then he swung slowly round on the revolving chair. His dark hair was dishevelled and his shirt unbuttoned almost to the waist. One look at him and she knew the truth. "It has to do with our Atlantic flight, hasn't it? What's Hooper done?"

His thick voice told her he was drunk. "He's put the dagger in, that's what he's done." He indicated an early edition of the *Los Angeles Times* lying on the carpet. "He's claiming he's got a witness overseas who heard us both talking the night before the flight."

She went hot and cold. "That's impossible. We were alone in my room."

"This witness claims she heard us talking from the corridor. It's that woman O'Malley. You remember her?"

"I don't understand. Why has Hooper waited so long?"

"He says the couple sold the pub shortly after we left and went over to England. When a woman in the village said the O'Malleys had gossiped about our conversation, Hooper put a man in England to look for them." The cords of his neck contracted as he lifted his glass and drank. Coughing, he gazed back at her. "I think the sonofabitch has known for some time. But he's waited until I said I was making another solo flight. You know why, don't you?"

She knew only too well. "I'll deny it, Dean. Before the sponsors pull out. I'll do it now."

He waved her back. "It's no good, baby. The phone's never stopped ringing all afternoon. Right now I haven't the sponsorship to fly a model aeroplane. I'm through, baby. Washed out."

She dropped on her knees by his chair. "No, you're not. I'll back your flight. I've got enough money now."

He gave a harsh laugh. "Do you know what it costs to lay on a hop like that?"

If she had felt he needed the flight before, she knew it was a matter of life and death now. "It won't be that expensive – not if you go to Alaska. We'll have no landing rights and fuel dumps to worry about. It'll just be the aircraft and fuel, and I can afford that. You can go ahead as before, Dean. I mean it." As shouts sounded outside and the door bell rang, she felt intense revulsion for a world that erected idols only to drag them down. "Let's show all the bastards how wrong they are."

The momentary crinkling of his eyes at her language showed that his sense of humour was not dead. At the same time he had never expressed his self-doubts more openly to her. "I can't risk your dough, honey. Maybe they are right and I am past it."

She threw her arms round him. "Don't talk like that! Show

them how wrong they are. Please. Dean. For my sake!"

The militancy of her defiance seemed to rally him for a moment. "You want it that bad, honey?"

She felt her marriage hung in the balance and her voice was fierce. "Yes. I want it. More than anything. I know it'll be hard for you but I'll deny everything that woman says. They've only got her word against mine. Things will soon settle down, particularly if people see you're preparing for another flight."

Outside there were more shouts for their attention and the door bell was ringing incessantly. She gripped his arm and shook him. "Phone for the police to clear the grounds. Then let's start making our plans. Come on, Dean! You've got to fight this."

He drained his glass and filled it again. Believing he was defeated, she drew back. At the window the brightness dimmed as two men tried to peer through the half-closed blinds. Pale with anger she was about to cry out to them when McArthur cursed, picked up the whisky bottle, and hurled it with all his strength.

There was a crash of glass and alarmed shouts outside. Elated she swung round to see McArthur reaching for the telephone.

NINETEEN

The sun-baked strip of sand stretched forward as far as the eye could see. The waves that lapped against it were little more than ripples: the Pacific was calm that day. A biplane rested on the hard sand above the high watermark. Behind it was a maintenance tent with an ambulance and fire engine standing at the ready. At the back of the beach half a dozen cars were parked at all angles on the sand dunes.

The plane was of curious configuration, its upper wing set further back along its fuselage than its lower. It was a Beechcraft Staggerwing with a Wright Cyclone engine. Delia had bought it second-hand from a middle-aged businessman whose bad heart had forced him to give up flying. Strongly built, it had a cabin that would hold four passengers: enough space to take the extra fuel tanks McArthur needed for his long Pacific flight.

With the help of Jimmy Carlile, he and Delia had been modifying and testing the Beechcraft for over three months. Needing a skilled engineer to carry out the modifications, McArthur had phoned Carlile the moment he had acquired the aircraft. Although the Texan had found a profitable job in Cincinnati, on hearing McArthur was planning another long-distance flight he had downed tools and caught the next train to Los Angeles. When told there were no sponsors and everything had to be done on a shoestring, he had hired help only when necessary. It had meant extra work for the Texan but his loyalty to McArthur had been in no way affected by the Atlantic flight revelations.

It had however affected the press coverage. Barely a dozen reporters were clustered round the Beechcraft and they came mostly from rural newspapers. The great city papers were hedging their bets, Delia thought as she stood alongside McArthur and Carlile. Tonight they would probably devote only one small paragraph to his departure but would show no embarrassment in using banner headlines again if his record attempt was successful.

One of the reporters was calling McArthur over for a last interview. As he walked towards them, a tall figure in his white overalls, Delia glanced at Carlile. "Is he going to be all right, Jimmy?"

If the ageing Texan had any doubts, he did not show them. "Why not? He hasn't been hitting the bottle lately, has he?"

"No, but he hasn't been sleeping well. At least not this last week."

"That doesn't mean anything. Everyone gets nervy before the big one. Weren't you?"

Having worked with the Texan for three months, she felt able to speak her thoughts. "It's not that. Somewhere along the line he's lost his confidence. He'd lost it before our Atlantic flight."

A residue of Carlile's old hostility showed as he gazed down at her. "Are you saying that's why you flew with him? To hold his hand?"

His sarcasm nettled her. "Of course I'm not. I was ambitious. I still am. But you can't deny that flight put him back on the map."

The grizzled Texan nodded at the sparse crowd. "Yeah. Right back."

She bit her lip. "It wasn't this way before Hooper found that Irish woman. Until then he got all the praise. You know that."

He turned to face her. "Is that gossip right? Did you do most of the flying?"

She wondered why he had waited so long to ask her. "Yes. He did his best but he was in great pain and what with the drugs he had to take, it all became too much for him in the end."

His tone changed. "Then you did a great job. Only as things have worked out, it might have been better if you'd stayed out of it."

"You mean for Dean?"

"Yeah."

"I don't know how you can say that. He's loved the publicity and the money. Anyway I believe he would have killed himself if he'd tried the flight alone. Even before he injured his arm."

"And yet you've encouraged him to fly this one."

She met his eyes squarely. "You didn't see him when Hooper's article was published. He's a proud man and it nearly destroyed him. He'd have drunk himself to death if I hadn't got him interested in flying again. I know it's a gamble but what other choice do I have?"

His nod killed her resentment. "Yeah, that's the picture I got. You are right, kid. You didn't have any choice."

Out at sea a line of cormorants were skimming the shining surface, searching for early morning fish. Her eyes moved to McArthur who was walking away from the reporters. He waved to her and Carlile. "O.K., you guys. Time to go."

They followed him to the cabin door. Carlile nodded at the stretch of beach ahead. "Remember the extra fuel you're carrying. Me and the men have checked the beach for a mile and a half – you'll see the marker on your right. If she hasn't lifted off by then, call it a day and throttle back. Otherwise you might hit a water course or shingle."

The extra forty gallons of fuel had been a last-minute decision by McArthur. The hundreds of gallons already pumped into the Beechcraft had given her only a hundred and fifty mile reserve. With weather forecasts impossible to obtain, McArthur had argued as he had argued in Ireland that it was better to take risks at take-off rather than over a friendless ocean.

With her personal fear of fire, Delia had been glad that Carlile had insisted on steel fuel tanks. They added to the aircraft's overall weight but in the event of a crash were marginally less likely to burst and hurl petrol over a red-hot engine.

McArthur nodded, clapped Carlile across his shoulders, then turned to Delia. "This is it, baby. Wish me luck."

She flung her arms round his neck. "Look after yourself, Dean. Good luck and Godspeed."

He met her eyes, winked, and then the cabin door closed.

The Wright Cyclone, notoriously a difficult engine to start, whined, wheezed, coughed, and finally burst into a roar and a cloud of oily grey-brown smoke. As Carlile drew Delia aside, the chocks were pulled away and the Beechcraft waddled forward. One or two desultory cheers were heard but in the main the reporters watched in silence.

The roar grew louder as McArthur advanced the throttle. As sand began pluming from its propeller, Delia turned to the intent Carlile. "I'm petrified, Jimmy. Have I done the right thing?"

He spoke without taking his eyes off the vibrating Beechcraft. "There wasn't anything else you could do. So stop worrying."

The heavily-loaded plane was picking up speed with alarming slowness. Its tail had not risen from the sand when it passed the first quarter-mile marker. Beside Delia, Carlile was now watching it through binoculars.

The seconds ticked away. Although the Beechcraft's engine sounded now like the bellow of a tortured steer, her tail did not rise until she was well past the half-mile marker. Delia gripped Carlile's arm. "He's overloaded her, Jimmy, hasn't he? He's not going to make it!"

The Texan did not answer but the rigidity of his arm betrayed his fear. She snatched the binoculars from him and focused them. She could see the Beechcraft's wheels pounding up and down on the packed sand but with no suggestion of parting company from it.

Another ten seconds passed. There were now shouts of alarm from the watching reporters and mechanics. Without ceremony, Carlile grabbed the glasses back from her. Angry with him, she found herself on tiptoe with her nails digging into her sweating palms. Even without glasses she could see that the distant plane had passed the one-mile marker but was still earthbound.

She tried to get the glasses back from Carlile but he shook her off. "How far's he got left?" she asked.

The Texan's voice was unnaturally calm. "He's past the mile and a quarter marker."

"Then he's not going to make it!" Her voice rose hysterically. "Stop it, Dean! You're going into the rough. Throttle back, for God's sake."

The distant bellow of the tortured engine was her only answer. Behind her the ambulance and fire tender crews were exchanging glances and starting up their engines.

The end came with terrifying suddenness. As if a giant hand had slapped down on her, the Beechcraft buckled and collapsed, an impact that could be felt through the ground. As its propeller shattered, the distant bellow turned into a piercing scream. The right wing struck the beach and with the engine still screaming, the entire aircraft went into a series of vicious ground loops, each one taking her nearer the sea. Fountains of spray rose as the watermark was reached, almost hiding the gyrating plane from sight. In her last convulsion, her engine dug into the waves and her fuselage rose high into the air and remained there.

All around Delia men were shouting and running for their cars. Sirens screaming, the ambulance and the fire tender raced past. Although Carlile was shouting at her and jerking her arm, she was staring at the wrecked Beechcraft with hypnotic fascination. With clouds of steam rising from it, she believed the fuel tanks had ruptured and a furnace was starting. Then Carlile swung her round. "Delia, for Chrissake! Are you coming or not?"

Stumbling, unable to speak or cry, she allowed him to drag her to their car. As he accelerated towards the wreck one thought dominated her shocked mind. It had been she who had encouraged him to make the flight. It was she who had made the disaster possible.

TWENTY

The nurse rose from her chair and came to the door. "Mrs McArthur?"

"Yes. How is my husband?"

"Have you seen Doctor Hardaker?"

"Yes. I've just come from his office. He says I can see Dean for a few minutes. Is he conscious?"

The nurse glanced back at the bed. "He was a few minutes ago although he keeps drifting off. Don't worry if you find he has no memory of the crash. He hasn't been out of shock long and he's had severe concussion."

"But there's no fracture, I believe?"

"Not to his head. But he has a broken collar bone and two fractured ribs."

McArthur's eyes were closed as she approached the bed. His face was unmarked except for a grazed cheek but his head was heavily bandaged. She leaned over him. "Dean! Can you hear me?"

His eyes opened slowly. At first they were muzzy as he stared at her. Then recognition seeped into them. His hoarse voice was very weak. "Hiya, baby. How's tricks?"

Suddenly she wanted to cry. "Hello, Dean. How do you feel?"

"How's a dog's dinner feel? They say I blew it. Was it bad?"

"Don't you remember anything?"

"Only bumping along that beach trying to get the goddamn thing to fly. What did I hit?"

"We don't know yet. But the undercarriage collapsed and you spun into the sea."

He tried to lift his head and failed. "Where's Jimmy?"

"He's in the waiting-room. They'd only let me see you

today. He said I had to give you a message, that you're the luckiest guy he knows. He's right, Dean. It's a miracle you got off so lightly."

His eyes, drawn with pain, suddenly looked confused. "He calls it lucky? To crash her on take-off like that?"

"What does that matter? You're alive. You can try again when you recover."

He lay motionless for a moment. She thought how pale his cheeks looked and for the first time noticed a couple of white threads in his beard. She was about to tiptoe away when his hoarse voice drew her back. "I'm sorry, honey."

"What for?"

"For blowing it like that. After all you did."

"That's the last thing to worry about. Forget it and just get well."

His confusion seemed to return. "Forget it?"

"Yes. There'll be another time." As his eyes closed and the nurse appeared in the doorway, she bent down and kissed him. "Go to sleep now. I'll be back again tomorrow."

She met Carlile in the corridor. Seeing her distress, he waited until they were in her car before asking his question. "How is he?"

She dabbed her eyes with a handkerchief. "He's still a bit woozy but I think he'll be all right."

"Then what are you crying for?"

She glanced at him defiantly. "Because I'm a stupid woman, I suppose."

"Don't give me that, kid. You're the girl who flew a Puss Moth to Cape Town and back. What's the problem?"

She glanced away. "I'm wondering what's going to happen to him now. I'm afraid he'll go to pieces."

"Mac? Never. He'll bounce back like a rubber ball."

Her lips began trembling again. "Jimmy, the press are going to crucify him. If they could hurt him so much before, think what they can do to him now."

The Texan scowled. "To hell with the press. Anyone can crash on take-off. It happens all the time."

"I know that but you're forgetting this flight was to prove he isn't slipping. Do you think people like Hooper are going to say it was just bad luck?" When Carlile did not answer, her tear-stained face pleaded with him. "Won't you stay a while longer, Jimmy? He's going to need every friend he's got and you're the kind who's good for him. And in any case we need someone to take care of the Beechcraft. I'll meet all your expenses."

He sat gazing at her for a moment, then motioned her to vacate the driving seat. "O.K., kid, but forget the expenses. They're shouting aloud for aero engineers at Boeing and anyway I like the climate here." As she showed her relief, he climbed in and switched on the engine. "Let's get you home. I reckon we both need a drink."

Paul phoned her shortly after Carlile left the villa. "Hello, Smudge. I've been trying to get you most of the day."

Her heart leapt at the sound of his voice. "Hello, Paul. Where are you?"

"In Philadelphia. Tell me – how's Dean?"

She told him. "I suppose he's been very lucky. But I know he's not going to see it that way." Her loyalty to McArthur, in conflict with her desire to confide in Paul, made her admission difficult. "It wouldn't have been so bad before these press articles. Now he'll feel he's only proved they are right."

"Has he said this?"

"He doesn't need to. It's already written on his face."

"What about your local newspapers? Have you had a chance to look at them yet?"

"I've seen the *Times*. They've just reported the crash and that Dean's been taken to hospital. I expect they'll keep their malice until he's well again. What do the East Coast papers say?"

"The ones I've seen have been sympathetic. You could be wrong about this, Smudge. After all the criticism Dean's had, he showed courage in attempting this flight. Fair-minded people can see this."

Her recent experience with the press had left her with little faith in its fair-mindedness. "No, the press loves trampling on its idols. Wait until Dean comes out of hospital and then see what happens."

He changed the subject. "I suppose this is going to affect your Australian plans?"

She winced. "I'm afraid it will. I can hardly leave for

England until he's fully recovered."

"Couldn't he go with you this time?"

"I can ask him, I suppose. Only he's dead against my doing another solo flight." Feeling she could not tell him why, she went on: "I still intend doing it but this does mean I'll have to put if off for a while."

"I can see that but it's a pity. Dad's really sold on you now and he's cooked up a scheme for you to fly around Australia after your arrival to show the flag."

"Show the flag?"

He laughed. "A euphemism for advertising his products. Very subtley done, of course. He wants me to organize the tour."

She gave a start. "Do you mean you'd go to Australia?"

"That's what he proposes. I'd meet you there and we'd fly to all the cities and major towns. He's prepared to give you an extra twenty thousand dollars if you agree."

At that moment she did not even think about the money, small fortune though it was. "How long would this take, Paul?"

"My estimate is six weeks. I couldn't be there any longer because of my commitments here. I've also got Gloria to think about."

"Wouldn't she be coming with you?"

"No. She's not keen on flying."

Six weeks on her own with Paul ... Flying round Australia with him ... It was like a dream come true. "How long can it wait, Paul?"

He hesitated. "You know how impatient my dad is. At a pinch I suppose I might stretch it to four months. But that would be the absolute limit."

"Do you mean my flight or the Australian tour at the end of it?"

"The Australian tour I'm afraid. In any case I'll be tied up myself after that."

She was making rapid calculations. The flight to Australia, unless she crashed and failed, should not take long but the preparations could take at least two months. Allowing for her to journey to England, she had little more than a month before leaving. "Will you explain things to your father, Paul, and ask him if he'll give me as long as possible? Tell him I'm desperately keen to do it."

"Yes, of course I will. I'm sorry to put pressure on you like this, Smudge, but you know how the Old Man's mind works."

She knew only too well. Sir Richard would use her and pay her well while she remained a world celebrity. If she allowed her image to fade, he would discard her like an old glove.

"I'll leave as soon as I can, Paul. But I can't leave Dean until he's fully recovered."

"I wouldn't want you to, Smudge. Nor would it be a good thing for your popularity if you did." His laugh was wry. "At times like this I wish my father wasn't such a high-pressure businessman."

"I know that, Paul. I'll be in touch the moment I feel I can get away." She paused, then could not hold back her wistful question. "I don't suppose there's any chance of you coming to the West Coast again soon, is there?"

"Not at the moment, I'm afraid. I'm up to my ears in work. But let's hope things work out better than you think and we can meet over in Australia."

She brushed a sleeve over her eyes. "I'll do my very best, Paul. Thanks for phoning about Dean. I'll be in touch."

Jimmy Carlile phoned her an hour later to let her know the salvage operations had been successful and the Beechcraft was safely on its way to the shed where he and his team had originally worked on it. "Can it be repaired, Jimmy?"

"It can be, kid. But it's going to be a hell of a big job. What do you want me to do?"

"I can't think now. Leave it until Dean's out of hospital and you've some idea what it's going to cost."

A dull headache forced her to bed early that night but although she took aspirins she could not sleep. Earlier in the day she had felt nothing but concern and sympathy for McArthur. Now, since receiving Paul's offer with its reminder of the price marriage demanded of her, all her old restlessness was back. To deny herself his sole company for six weeks was a pain that seemed too sharp to bear and one that drove away her sense of fairness and responsibility. At that moment, lying there in the darkness, she felt she would give ten years of her life to be free and in charge of her own destiny again.

TWENTY ONE

She laid an envelope down on the table alongside McArthur. "These arrived this morning. They're mostly afterthoughts from the monthly aviation magazines." When he made no comment, she went on: "They're not critical. Most of them recognize the heavy fuel load you needed to carry on a long ocean flight like that."

He pushed the envelope away. "Forget what they say. What are you doing tonight? Coming out with me or not?"

It was over six weeks since his crash, and her worst fears had been realized. His physical wounds had healed but not his mind. It did not matter that the press on the whole had shown sympathy and even admiration for his courage. His pride had suffered damage that no comfort from her or anyone else could alleviate. The only solace he seemed to get was from alcohol and 'with Prohibition ended' liquor was available from the hundreds of bars that had sprung up almost overnight.

At first she had felt it her duty to go out with him but had soon found she could not stand the pace. Whereas once alcohol had made him good-humoured, now it made him aggressive. Twice he had become involved in fights when she was with him and on the second occasion the police had been called in. After this second fight she realized her presence made no difference. In fact his behaviour made her suspect that in some perverse way he showed more aggression when she was there to witness it.

Paul had phoned her twice during this period and the second time she had confessed her problem. "I just don't know what to do, Paul. I don't seem able to help him and yet if I go to Europe I'm afraid he might crack up completely."

"You are sure he won't go over there with you?"

"Quite sure. He just flies into a temper if I mention it. In any case what would he do while I was in Australia?"

"Couldn't he join us there? It would at least get him away from the crowd he's with now."

Even to Paul she could not admit the reason McArthur was against her second flight. "It's no use. I can't even talk to him about it."

"Then what do you want me to do, Smudge? Shall I tell dad you can't manage it, at least not this year?"

She had felt physically sick at the possibility of losing the offer. "Couldn't you wait just a little longer, Paul? Something might still happen to change his mind."

He had been unable to hide his doubts. "Dad's such an impatient character. But I'll do my best."

She was recalled to the present by McArthur's question. "I asked if you were coming out with me tonight."

It was not easy to hide the resentment her thoughts had evoked. "Can't we stay in tonight? It's weeks since we had a night at home together."

"And do what?" he asked.

She gave a helpless laugh. "What do people do when they stay at home? Listen to the radio. Read books. Even talk to one another."

His expression suggested a sarcastic reply. Instead he said: "So you're not coming?"

"I can't, Dean. I can't drink like you."

He drained his wineglass, rose, and made for his room. "O.K. I suppose in the long run it's the best thing."

"What does that mean?"

When he did not answer, she followed him into the room. "I asked what you meant by that remark."

He was standing before the dressing-table adjusting his tie. "I meant I'd better get used to being alone. Any day now you'll be off again to England, won't you?"

Her face set. "That's not fair. I put back all my plans so you could attempt the Alaskan flight. You can't expect me to put them off forever."

He shrugged. "It's a pity you wasted your time, isn't it, for all the good it's done."

With her reservoir of compassion almost exhausted, there

was more impatience than sympathy in her voice. "For God's sake stop punishing yourself and everybody else for what happened. It wasn't your fault. When will you accept that?"

He made no comment. His image, thrown back at her by the dressing-table mirror, added to her resentment. He looked fifty instead of forty, she thought, with his pouched eyes and thickening waistline. "You're killing yourself with all this drinking," she said. "Don't you realize that?"

He gave an indifferent shrug and reached for his jacket. "There are worse ways of dying, baby."

"That's childish and stupid. Don't you owe me something? We are married, you know."

He paused, then turned, his eyes bitter with dislike. "Yeah, so we are. I guess at times I forget that."

"And what does that mean?"

"You telling me you don't know?"

"All right, you want a child. So do I. Only I want you to wait until I've achieved my ambitions. Is that so much to ask?"

"Not a bit, baby. All husbands wait for kids until their wives get to the top of the tree. It's the goddamned order of things."

His sarcasm brought out her own aggression. "You hate my ambitions, don't you? You think it's something only men should have. You'd prefer one of those little yes women, wouldn't you?"

He shrugged on his jacket. "One thing is for sure, baby. I don't have one."

"No, you haven't. I've the same rights to fulfil myself that you have."

"And you don't think having a baby is fulfilling yourself?"

"No. For some women, perhaps. But not for me. I want more out of life."

"Like flying to Cape Town and Australia. You think that makes you a full woman?"

His inference, the unfairness of his views, combined to drive all restraint from her. "It's made you into a full man, hasn't it? Record breaking's all you've ever done." Ignoring his expression, she went on: "You don't want me to go on breaking records, do you? Not now."

The sudden silence was as loud as an explosion. When he spoke his voice was hoarse. "Why don't I want you to, baby?"

Suddenly realizing she was on the edge of the brink, she drew back. "It doesn't matter. Drop it."

His eyes were alive with suspicion. "I asked why I don't want you to break any more records."

Turning on her heel, she walked from the bedroom. "I don't want to talk about it any more. I'm going to take a bath."

For a moment she thought he was going to run after her and force her to answer. Instead he cursed and made for the front door. A few seconds later a car engine broke into life and tyres squealed destructively down the road.

For the next week Delia saw little of him except at mealtimes and some of them he missed. To Mrs Levinsky's clear disapproval, he slept in a spare bedroom, an event that more than anything else told Delia that the rift between them was rapidly growing into a chasm. While upset on the one hand, she could not pretend to herself that the move was wholly unwelcome. In the past she had enjoyed his love-making but that had been with a relatively sober lover. A lover almost too drunk to know what he was doing was another matter, particularly when she was now practising birth control herself. Added to his resentment at her precautions, there had also been physical problems that had caused her both embarrassment and anger. Now she could sleep with neither.

It was over a week before they went out together again. The event was a small party Len and Cynthia Downsley had invited them to weeks before their recent quarrel. The Downsleys were one of the few local couples who in Delia's eyes were friends of theirs in spite of rather than because of their fame, and on any other occasion she would have enjoyed the evening.

Instead the party proved a disaster. The Downsleys had two children, a boy and a girl, and it was not long before McArthur began making innuendoes about childless marriages. At first they were low key enough for only Delia to notice their significance but as McArthur drained glass after glass of whisky they became pointed enough for everyone at the party to grasp their meaning.

By eleven she had had enough and pleaded a headache as an excuse to leave. She thought McArthur would stay and let someone else drive him home – his usual custom on such occasions – but tonight for some perverse reason he chose to go back with her. Determined not to let him drive, she made sure she was first in the driver's seat. He stood at the door staring at her. "What's the big idea? Move over."

"No," she said. "I'm driving. You're too drunk."

When he cursed and tried to enter the car, she pushed him back. "I don't intend to let myself be killed or spend the night in a police cell. Either I drive or I'll ask someone at the party to take me."

Seeing she was adamant he walked round the car and dropped into the passenger seat. Neither spoke a word during the fifteen minutes it took them to reach home. As she entered the drive and switched off the engine, he turned to her, "You're in a bitch of a mood, aren't you?"

Her voice was cold with anger. "What do you expect from a bitch? That's what you've been calling me all night, isn't it?"

"What the hell are you talking about?"

"I'm the bitch who won't give you children. Everyone in California must know it by this time. It'll probably be in the gossip columns tomorrow."

He followed her into the villa. In the hall she turned on him. "Don't you ever do that to me again! What we do or don't do about children is our private affair. I won't have it talked about among our friends. Are you listening to me?"

The intensity of her anger sobered him. "For Christ's sake, stop exaggerating."

"Don't you dare tell me I'm exaggerating. You've done nothing but criticize me ever since you had that crash. You're taking it out on me, yet I'm the person who paid for everything. Have you forgotten that?"

Although he had been surprised at her attack, his bitterness now began to feed from it. "You're not going to let me forget that, are you?"

"That's a lie. You're the one who can't forget it. You feel you failed and so you lash out at me. Well, don't! Tonight's finished it for me. I've had enough."

"You've had enough? What about me? I'm married and I

have to sleep in a single bed. All because my wife puts her goddamned ambitions before her womanhood.''

They were enemies now, each doing his best to hurt the other. ''You sleep in a single bed out of choice. Like a sulking child. Sometimes I think that's what I'm married to. A man who can't face what's happened and drinks to forget it.''

His cheeks went chalk white. ''You cow!''

''If I'm a cow, you've made me one. I got you across the Atlantic and you took all the credit for it. How would you have felt if I'd done that? I had to take on the Cape flight to prove myself and yet you tried to stop me. Now you're trying to stop me going to Australia. What's the matter with you? Are you scared they'll think I'm a better man than you?''

Her taunt seemed to explode all the frustrations of his failures. As he cursed and moved forward, she believed he was going to strike her. Instead he grabbed her, swung her up in his arms and carried her into their bedroom. Although she kicked and struggled he crossed over to the bed and flung her down on it. ''You bitch,'' he said hoarsely. ''I'll show you what kind of man you are.''

Before she could rise, he dropped on top of her. One hand ripped open the front of her dress, the other dipped hard into her groin. Her cry was one of outrage. ''Let me go, damn you! Let me go!''

He was sobbing like a man possessed. His bearded face searched for her mouth while he fumbled and tore at her clothing. She clawed at his cheeks with her nails but he drove her arms away. Her head turned from side to side in a desperate attempt to avoid him but his mouth found her lips and clamped on them while his knees forced her legs apart. She fought like a tigress but his weight and strength pinned her heaving body down. When pain stabbed her she knew further resistance was useless. With a moan she allowed her body to relax.

The madness seemed to leave him after he sprang his seed. He tried to kiss her unresponsive face and when she turned away he dropped beside her. He lay silent for awhile as if trying to understand what had happened. Then he turned and touched her icy cheek. ''Baby, I'm sorry. I don't know what came over me.''

Her voice came from an outraged stranger. "Go away. I don't want to see you or talk to you. You disgust me. Go away."

Suddenly he sounded panic-stricken. "Honey, I didn't mean to hurt you. Something came over me ... oh Christ, I don't know what it was. But I'm sorry."

She turned her cold face back to him. "I know what it was. And if I have a baby because of it, you'll never see me again. Or the child. I promise you that."

"But I was drunk, baby. I didn't mean it. Honest to God I didn't."

"Go away," she said again. "I can't bear to be in the same room with you. Go away."

He sat a moment looking at her, then slowly rose and went out. She heard him enter the bathroom and the flush of water followed. A couple of minutes later he returned to the bedroom door and gazed at her. When she neither moved nor spoke, he shook his head and turned away.

She lay motionless, her eyes on the dark ceiling. Once again she heard his car start up and drive away. This time, however, there was no squeal of tyres. He drove away slowly, like an ashamed man dragging his feet.

She lay there until the sound of the car died away. Then she went into the bathroom, removed her torn clothes, and gave herself a douche. Still trembling, she threw on a dressing-gown, poured herself a large whisky, and sat huddled in front of the electric fire. With her mind a battlefield, she had only one clear thought. Her first act in the morning would be to call Paul and tell him she was ready to leave for England on the next available ship.

TWENTY TWO

Delia glanced at the clock on the living-room wall. She was wondering what time Paul arrived at his office. She knew he had recently bought a house in Philadelphia but she did not want to call his home. Gloria might answer the phone and that morning, for all kinds of reasons, she did not want to speak to Gloria.

She wandered to the window. It had rained during the night and birds were grubbing for worms on the lawn. As she waited her impatience grew. Allowing for the east to west coast time difference, Paul would surely be in his office now. She decided to give him ten more minutes and lit herself a cigarette.

She found herself wondering where McArthur had spent the night. The thought was a catalyst, instantly recalling his behaviour the previous night. As her cheeks burned with shame and anger she decided she would contact her lawyer later in the day to find out if under Californian law she had a case for divorce.

She waited until her cigarette had burned down and then phoned Paul's office. "Hello. My name is Delia McArthur. I would like to speak to Mr Paul Findlay, please."

To her relief Paul was there. Although he was clearly pleased to hear from her, she imagined a slight diffidence in his voice. "Hello, Delia. This is a nice surprise. What can I do for you?"

"Paul, listen. I can accept your father's offer. Something's happened: I'll explain later. Will you let him know right away?"

The line went silent. Suddenly her mouth turned dry. "Paul? What is it?"

She heard him sigh. "I've got bad news for you, Delia. He

133

was on the phone two nights ago and he mentioned your trip. He said he couldn't wait any longer and that I'd better let you know so you could make other plans."

She felt as if she had been struck across the face. "Does he mean the tour round Australia or the record attempt?"

"Both, I'm afraid. I'm desperately sorry, Smudge, but that's my father. If people don't jump when he cracks the whip, he soon gets impatient."

She tried to steady herself. "Does this mean all my sponsors have pulled out?"

"I don't know about that but as Dad was the one who got them together, I suppose there could be a few problems there."

She knew too well what he meant. If Sir Richard had pulled out the others would feel he had good reason. His voice broke into her misery. "Are you very disappointed, Smudge?"

She wanted to tell him she was broken-hearted. Instead she managed a laugh. "It's a blow, yes. But I'll get over it."

"What will you do now?"

She wished to God she knew. "I'll think of something. I suppose a few people over there must still remember me."

He sounded relieved. "The whole country remembers you. There must be dozens of firms who'll be interested. If I can do anything to help, you'll let me know, won't you?"

She was glad he could not see her tears. "Yes, of course I will. But you've done enough for me already, Paul. I'll always be grateful."

She could not remember afterwards how their conversation ended. She was still sitting by the phone when Mrs Levinsky arrived. "What's the matter with you, luv? You look as if you've seen a ghost."

She decided to tell it then and there. "Don't prepare any more meals for my husband, Mrs Levinsky. He's left home."

Mrs Levinsky looked both shocked and disapproving. "You mean for good?"

"Yes. We'll probably be getting a divorce."

"What've you had? A quarrel?"

"Yes. A bad one."

"You don't get divorced over quarrels, luv. Not unless they're about money."

"It wasn't about money," she said.

"Then everything can be patched up. Always remember there's two sides to quarrels and husbands aren't that easy to find. Not husbands like yours."

Delia tried to smile. "What's so special about mine?"

The woman shrugged her ample shoulders. "He's fun, luv, that's what's special. If you'd been married to the miserable old sod I had for thirty years, you'd know what I mean."

Jimmy Carlile phoned that afternoon. "Hello, kid. I'd like a chat with Mac about these repairs. Is he home?"

"No," she said.

"Then get him to phone me as soon as he's back, will you?"

She knew Carlile would have to know. "He won't be coming back, Jimmy. We'd a bad quarrel last night and he left. I thought that perhaps he'd spent the night in your apartment."

"No. I haven't seen him for two days. So you don't know where he is?"

"I can take a guess. Probably with his latest girl-friend."

"Aw, come on, kid. Mac's not like that any more. Not since he met you."

"Who told you that?" she asked bitterly. "Dean?"

"It's true. He has changed. He told me so one night. And he'd no cause to lie to me."

Her anger held no brief for reason or fair play. "You must be the only person he hasn't lied to." Her tone changed. "I'm sorry, Jimmy. You're his friend: I shouldn't drag you into this."

"That's O.K., kid. Anyway, he'll be back with you soon. You've got to say that about the guy. He never bears grudges."

Everyone sees the good side of him but me, she thought bitterly. "You don't understand, Jimmy. It was I who told him to get out."

There was a short troubled silence. Then: "I'm sorry. Can I help?"

"Not really. But if you find out where he is, you might let me know. I'll need his address for my lawyer."

"Is it as bad as that, kid?"

"Yes, Jimmy. It's very bad."

"Aw, hell. I'm sorry. I'll start looking for him right away. What about the plane? Shall I carry on repairing it?"

She suddenly felt very tired. "I gave it to him so you'd better ask him about that. I don't expect he'll ever fly it again but as he's nearly through his money, he'll probably want to sell it. So I'm sure he'll want you to carry on."

"O.K. I'll take care of it. And you hang on, kid. It'll all come right. Trust your Uncle Jim."

She tried to laugh. "All right, Uncle Jim. I'll hang on."

An hour later she drove Mrs Levinsky to the shops. As she drew up outside a greengrocer, a newstand poster on the opposite side of the road caught her eyes. "AIR SWEETHEARTS QUARREL. BREAK-UP SOON?

Mrs Levinsky had not seen it. "You stay here and watch the car, luv. I'll be as quick as I can."

She watched the woman's ample body disappear into the shop, then turned to gaze at the poster again. She wanted to cross the road and buy a paper but suddenly her legs felt unequal to the task. There would be no way of keeping their conflict a private matter now. The wolves had caught the scent and were hot on their heels.

It was three days before Carlile contacted her again. This time he came to the villa. "Hello, kid. I've found Mac."

She led him into the living-room and motioned him into an armchair. "Feel like a drink?"

He shook his grizzled head. "No. I guess I've seen too much of it today."

She poured herself a whisky, then dropped into a chair opposite him. "Is he that bad?"

"Yeah, he's bad all right. It took me a couple of hours to sober him up."

"Where is he?"

"In a crummy hotel down town. He wouldn't say why he's there. Maybe it's to keep away from his friends."

"Why should he do that?" she asked bitterly. "Everyone knows he's not a member of the Temperance Society."

When he did not answer she took another look at him and saw he was wearing a faint air of embarrassment. "He told you what happened, didn't he?"

He hesitated, then shifted uneasily. "Yeah. I guess he did."

"Well. Can you understand how I feel about him now?"

He cleared his throat. "Yeah, I suppose I can."

"Suppose? What does that mean?"

"I mean I can understand."

She gazed at him contemptuously. "I don't believe you. You're a man. You don't think a husband can rape his wife, do you?"

He made a gesture of protest. "No, it's not that. It's just that Mac's never been the kind of guy who's brutal to women. It's not his style."

"How do you know that?"

"I've known him a long time, kid, and I've known his friends."

"You mean his women!"

"Some were, yes. But no one ever said he was cruel."

Her laugh was bitter. "Maybe he's just that way to his wives. Or are you hinting it was my fault?"

There was a film of sweat on the Texan's forehead. "No. Mac never said that. It's just that this time some things have hurt him more than we thought."

"What things?"

"Things like those articles saying he didn't pull his weight during your Atlantic hop and that he wasn't up to it any more. I reckon that caused his crash. He knew that if he'd pulled up when he ran out of runway they'd have said he was yellow."

She nodded. "I guessed that. But does he have to go on a bender ever since? Isn't that only proving them right?"

"Things affect different people different ways, kid. A man isn't always to blame for that."

"Not for raping a woman?" she asked. His frown and hesitation made her lean forward. "You said *things* had upset him. What you really meant was my refusal to have a baby. He mentioned that too, didn't he?"

He avoided her eyes. "Yes, he mentioned it."

"And that was his excuse for raping me? Right?"

He evaded her question. "He's in a hell of a state, kid. He's a proud man and this disgrace is killing him. I don't think he knows what he's doing half the time."

She gave an exclamation of disgust. "If he cut out the drinking he might give himself a chance. Real men don't buckle this way. They stand up and fight."

His eyes, very blue under their greying brows, were suddenly full of reproach. "There you're wrong, kid. I've known Mac a long time. He's been a playboy and sometimes he's been a fool, but he's never been a quitter. Nor has he ever been vicious. This thing has to be killing him to make him act like this."

"So what? Am I supposed to be sorry and forgive him?"

His glance made her feel uncomfortable. "That's something only you can decide. But I've always figured you as the loyal kind who don't walk out easily."

"Rape," she demanded.

"Yeah. I know that's terrible. But I know the guy loves you. Sometimes I think you're the only girl he's ever loved."

"Rape," she repeated.

He sighed. "O.K. You can't forgive him. But does that mean you won't help him get his pride and self-respect back?"

"How can I do that? I gave him a chance and what happened? Your friendship's blinding you to the truth, Jimmy. His nerve's gone. He's finished. Period."

He winced. "You could be right: I don't know. But there's one way you could help him."

"What way?"

He lit a cigarette before replying. "You could do another dual flight with him. Like you promised you would."

She gave a start. "Did he suggest this?"

"Christ, no. Even drunk Mac's a proud man. He'd wait until hell froze over before asking you. I'm suggesting it. It's the one way you might save him."

Outrage was still denying her any other emotion. "Why should I?"

"That's something only you can answer."

"Then I'll give my answer. No! And I've plenty of reasons. How could I work with a drunk? And even if he sobered up, how could we work without quarrelling or without him believing he can come back and live with me as if nothing had happened? Lastly, even if it did work, why should I let him have all the glory again?"

The Texan shook his head. "No, kid! Not this time."

"Why not?" she demanded.

"Because he's ashamed. I've never seen a guy so ashamed."

"So he damn well should be. I can't forgive him, Jimmy. No woman could. Anyway, I don't believe a dual flight would help him now. Those articles have turned the tables. If we broke a record now, no one would believe he'd pulled his weight."

He gazed at her, then sighed and rose. "O.K. Only I had to try. Mac and I go back a long way together."

She rose with him. "I know that, Jimmy. For your sake I'd like to help. But I just can't."

He walked to the window and gazed at the crowd of reporters who had been camped outside since early morning. "They're sure to have another go at me. What shall I tell them?"

All her frustration came to the boil. "Tell them my private life's my own business and they can all go to hell. Tell them I said it."

He gave her a lopsided grin. "That's fine with me. Shall I let you know from time to time how Mac's getting on?"

She avoided his eyes. "Yes, why not? In any case I hope it's not going to change things between us, Jimmy. I wouldn't like that."

She thought he hesitated. "No, kid. That won't happen. I'll be around. Take care."

The newsmen milled around him as he stepped outside. Watching from the window she saw him make some curt remark that brought shouts of protest from them as he walked to his car. Her expression was troubled as she turned away. She hoped she had not lost the respect of the shrewd but affable Texan.

It was that night when she lay thinking about Carlile's visit that the elf of conscience, planted in her by her Northern upbringing, made its small voice heard at last. What had been those words in her wedding vows? In sickness and in health ... for richer or poorer ... She had been happy enough to share Dean's triumphs. Did that not confer on her the obligation to share his misfortunes too?

There was no denying that whatever had happened since, she would have known nothing of fame or fortune without him. Meeting him had changed every aspect of her life. There would have been no Atlantic flight, no ticker tape welcome, no Cape Town flight, no world fame. He might not have engineered her success but he had been the catalyst that had made that success possible.

Then, as always, her ambition rose in conflict against her conscience. Her partnership with him had not been one-sided. Without her he would never have crossed the Atlantic and reburnished, if only for a time, his fading star. On a strictly one to one count she was not in his debt. And yet ...

Although she had dismissed Carlile's suggestion of a dual flight with contempt, she was now able to consider it objectively. She did not deceive herself. She knew that if the Australian tour with Paul were still on offer, she would not be giving a dual flight with Dean a second thought. But although she believed she could still get sponsors for the Australian flight itself, she felt oddly unenthusiastic about making the effort.

She was puzzled why. Perhaps she had waited too long and blunted her keenness. Or was it because of the ever-growing number of pioneer flights that had been taking place recently? Success no longer meant banner headlines, comments were growing more critical, and although she had the great advantage of being a girl, there was still no guarantee that success would win her the acclaim given her after her Cape flight (perhaps the thinking that was behind Sir Richard's cancellation?). The public had suddenly become jaded and something new was needed to stimulate their appetite.

It was then she remembered an article she had read a few days ago in the *Aviation News*. At the time it had excited her but the subsequent events of her personal life had driven it from her mind. Now she felt her pulse stirring. It was not something she could attempt alone: she had no experience of high-speed racing. But McArthur had: in his early days he had taken part in many aviation races. In fact she could think of no one more professionally competent to share such a contest with her.

The more she thought about the idea, the more her

excitement grew. Perhaps this was the answer, the one project that could make her ambition and her conscience allies instead of enemies. With its possibilities growing in her mind by the moment, she found herself impatient for the morning when she could present her idea to Carlile and to Paul.

TWENTY THREE

It was only a few minutes past nine a.m. the following morning when she drove up to the large shed which housed the Beechcraft. Seeing there was a hired hand working with Carlile, she called the Texan outside. When he reached her, she wasted no time on preliminaries. "I've got an idea, Jimmy. Something that might help both Dean and me."

Carlile showed relief. "That's wonderful, kid. What is it?"

"I'll tell you in a moment." Her voice hardened. "I'd need promises from him first. He'd have to swear not to touch another drop of liquor, he'd work under my conditions, and he'd do it on the understanding we were business partners and nothing more. If he broke just one condition, I'd drop the project like a red-hot brick."

Something in the Texan's gaze made her flush. "All right, I sound hard. Don't blame me for that. It's what he's made me."

Carlile nodded quietly. "O.K., kid. I've got the score. What's the project?"

"It's a dual flight but a special kind. It has to be, after my Cape flight and Dean's fall from grace. Have you read anything about the proposed England-Australia air race?"

The Texan gave a start. "No. Who's behind it?"

"It seems next year is the centenary of Melbourne and an Australian magnate, Sir MacPherson Robertson, is prepared to offer fifteen thousand to the first crew to reach Melbourne. It's still on the drawing-boards in England – that's probably why there hasn't been much talk about it over here – but the *Aviation News* seems confident it'll come off. If it does, there are sure to be entries from all over the world, so it'll attract big publicity."

Carlile was showing both excitement and admiration. "Kid, that's a terrific idea. It's right up Mac's street. Does he know anything about it?"

"I shouldn't think so. He's hardly been in a condition to know much about anything recently, has he?"

He ignored her bitter remark. "How would you set it up?"

"If he agreed to my conditions, I might go to de Havillands in England. They're reported to be already building a racer to compete. I'm hoping you'd come over with Dean. Apart from our needing you as an engineer, you'd help to keep him out of trouble. Would you come?"

The Texan shrugged. "Why not? I'll be looking for a job once the Beechcraft's repaired."

"Good. Then will you put it to Dean and see what he says?"

"Sure I will. I'll go and find him right away." Carlile hesitated. "Only you'll need to talk to him about the details yourself, won't you?"

She knew he meant the personal details. "Yes. If he's interested, tell him to come round to the villa about seven tonight. If he's not interested or you can't find him, then give me a ring."

The Texan was already divesting himself of his overalls. "I'm on my way, kid. Whatever happens, I'll call you this afternoon."

McArthur arrived just after six-thirty. Seeing who was in the car, the reporters still camped outside the villa made a rush for him. Their shouted questions, asking if his visit meant a reconciliation, brought Delia to the window. She watched his tall figure brush angrily through them and make for the door.

To avoid a confrontation with the newsmen herself, Delia asked the unperturbable Mrs Levinsky to let McArthur in. For a moment there were loud shouts and a scuffle, then the voices quietened as the housekeeper slammed the door. A few seconds later McArthur entered the living-room.

He was wearing a fawn sweater over an open-necked shirt and her first thought was how unwell he looked. There were pouches beneath his eyes, his cheeks looked gaunt, and the sweater hung loosely from his broad shoulders. The glance he gave her was sullen with shame and embarrassment. "Jimmy said you wanted to see me about some race from England to Australia. Is that right?"

At least, she thought, he was sober. She motioned him to sit down. "Yes. I thought it might interest you. Has he given you my conditions?"

"Yeah, I've got them."

"Do you agree to them? I want to know that first of all, otherwise there's no point in discussing anything."

He gazed at her, then sank into an armchair and lit a cigarette. "I don't drink and we're just business partners. Right?"

"Yes. Only there's no need for the press to know this."

He lifted an eyebrow. "You don't think they'd find out?"

"Not if we act sensibly." She went on before he could reply: "I might want a divorce when the race is over but until it is I don't want reporters pestering us about our private lives."

"You won't be able to stop them. Not if we live apart."

She knew he was probably right. "Perhaps we can live in different rooms in the same hotel. But that's something we can work out later. What about your drinking? Are you going to be able to stay off it that long?"

For a moment his tone was hostile. "You'll have to wait and find out, won't you?"

"No, I want to know now. I don't want any more scenes with you, at work or anywhere else."

From his expression it was clear he knew to what she was referring. "I want to enter this race as much as you. So you can forget about the drinking. What plans have you made so far?"

"I thought I'd first go over to England and do that *Daily Mail* lecture tour. I owe it to them and the money will help to buy the plane. In the meantime I suggest you and Jimmy finish repairing the Beechcraft. Then the two of you could come over and help me assess this new plane de Havilland are building. If we feel it is the right horse for the course, I'll order one and we'll play it from there."

He was shaking his head. "O.K. but for one thing. I'll buy the ship."

Carlile had already told her that for the sake of his pride he wanted to share the cost of the enterprise but she could not avoid her suspicions. "You do realize this is a joint project and has to be announced as such? That this time I'm not going to be the junior partner?"

"Yeah, yeah, I know all that. You're going to get the top billing. But I'm going to buy the ship. Otherwise the deal's off."

She bit her lip. "No one's getting a top billing. We're going into this as co-entrants and co-pilots." For a moment her bitterness spasmed, as she had known it would. "Where are you going to get the money from? Hasn't it all gone on booze and parties?"

Resentment edged his voice. "I've still got some left. And there's the Beechcraft. It should bring a good price."

It was on the tip of her tongue to ask who had bought the Beechcraft but decided that would be too bitchy. "All right, you sell it and buy the new racer. But if you let the press or anyone else know about it so they believe it's your race, I'll walk out and tell the world why."

If she needed proof of his desire to rehabilitate himself it showed in the way he held back his temper. "Nobody will be told, for Chrissake. You can say you bought it, if you like."

There was one thing that had to be said and now she saw how anxious he was to enter the race, she could not resist a stab of malice. "You do realize there is one thing that could knock the entire project on the head, don't you?"

"What's that?"

"If your rape made me pregnant. I wouldn't have an abortion, so we'd have to call the whole thing off."

He winced. "When will you know?"

"In just over two weeks."

He drew in smoke. "Does that mean you're going to wait until then?"

"No, I'll write to the *Mail* and I'll ask de Havilland for this new aircraft's specifications. But I can't make any firm commitment until I know my condition. If all's well, I'll get in touch with you or Jimmy to arrange a fresh talk. I take it you'll be spending your days with Jimmy now?"

"Yeah. The sooner we get the Beechcraft shipshape the better."

She rose. "Then you'll be hearing from me one way or the

other.'' She paused, wondering what tone and words to use to conclude the meeting. ''If I'm not pregnant, let's try to make it work. It'll be the biggest race in aviation history and it would be a terrific feather in our caps if we could win it.''

His matter-of-fact manner could not disguise his eagerness. ''What have I to lose? O.K. Let's see what we can do.''

Satisfied, she watched him press out his cigarette and rise. Without attempting to touch her or to shake hands, he went to the door. There his mood seemed to change and he turned back. ''You don't need to worry about me, baby. Flying's my life and life isn't much without it. I appreciate your offer, particularly after the way I behaved. I want you to know that.''

His chastened words caught her by surprise. Before she could speak, the door closed and he had gone.

Two weeks later, to her immense relief, Delia had a period. Wanting to waste no more time she put a phone call through to the repair shed. To avoid any tension between herself and McArthur, she spoke to Carlile.

''You can tell Dean everything's all right and we can go ahead with our plans. I've also received details of this new de Havilland racer. At the moment they're only building three but they say they're prepared to build more if orders come in.''

''What are her specifications, kid?''

''The brochure says she's a twin-engined, two-seater, low-wing cantilever monoplane. She's going to have two special Gipsy Six racing engines of two hundred and thirty hp each, with controllable pitch aircrews. The undercarriage will be completely retractable and the wing sections will be very thin because of stressed skin construction. The brochure says that because the Comet's being specially designed for the race, she'll meet all the conditions and regulations governing it.''

Carlile had all the caution of the professional engineer. ''Isn't she going to be underpowered with two hundred and thirty hp engines?''

''The brochure says not. They're giving her low-powered engines deliberately to increase her range but they still guarantee a top speed of two hundred mph. Don't forget they're in-line engines and the streamlining is like nothing you've seen before."

"What's the range? Do they say?"

"No but they claim it'll be exceptional. It ought to be. Most of the fuselage is one long fuel tank with the in-line cockpits just in front of the tail."

"Did they send an illustration?"

"Yes. She looks beautiful, Jimmy. A real thoroughbred."

Carlile sounded amused. "You're gone on her, aren't you, kid?"

"She's a racer, Jimmy. Something I've never flown before. And she's made in England. I'd like to win in an English plane."

The Texan laughed. "You're a jingoist, kid. I always knew it. What price are they asking?"

"Five thousand pounds. If she does all they say, she'll be cheap at the price."

"Have they sent you the race conditions?"

"Yes. It's open to anybody provided their aircraft conforms with the requirements of the International Commission on Aerial Navigation. That includes take-off run, climbing ability and structural strength. There are two sections, a speed race and a handicap. Everyone has to land at five check-points, Baghdad, Allahabad, Singapore, Charlesville and of course Melbourne. There are also plenty of intermediate check-points. Replacements on route are permitted and every plane has to carry lifebelts and three days provisions."

"What about the crews?"

"There's no limit to their number but every competing pilot has to give evidence of his competence. We shouldn't have any problems there."

"So what's our next move, kid?"

"I'm going to put in a provisional order for a Comet. In the meantime you'd better bring Dean round one night to talk the whole thing over. How long will it be before the Beechcraft's ready for sale?"

"Quite a while yet, kid. It's slow work with only two pairs of hands."

"That's all right. I still have my *Daily Mail* lecture tour to make. Once you've sold the Beechcraft you can both meet me in England and we can assess the Comet. If she's everything they say, we can put in a firm order and start planning our race."

"It sounds fine, kid, only can we leave our order that long?"

"They say so. They say they'll take new orders until the end of the year."

"O.K. I'll speak to Mac and phone you back. What's your best night?"

"Any night will suit me. Make it as quick as you can, Jimmy."

Her eyes were bright when she replaced the phone. At that moment she had no thought of the problems she might be making for herself by sharing another flying venture with McArthur. That die was cast. Her only thought was that next year she would be taking part in the greatest air race the world had ever known. It was a prospect that filled her with enormous exhilaration.

TWENTY FOUR

The red-painted Comet looked as futuristic as a space rocket beside the square biplanes lining the airfield perimeter. The ferry pilot who had brought it to Brook Lane was talking to a small group of people standing on the tarmac apron in front of the hangar. Among them were Delia and McArthur, the latter wearing flying overalls. The other members of the party were Jimmy Carlile and Alan Wright.

Bromley, the de Havilland ferry pilot, was a lanky young man sporting a fair moustache and a public-school accent. He was directing his comments to McArthur. "To sum it up, sir, she's fast, she can go a long way, but she's a bit tricky to fly. Shall we give her a go?"

"What are we waiting for?" McArthur turned to Delia. "O.K., baby. Let's find out if she's worth our money."

"Take your time," she told him. "Get the feel of her before you take over."

McArthur nodded, glanced at Carlile, then followed the pilot to the streamlined Comet with its low-slung engines. Delia and the two engineers followed a few paces behind.

The roof of the greenhouse-type cockpit, far back along the fuselage, was opened and the two pilots climbed inside. Half a minute later the Gypsy engines coughed and fired. As the chocks were pulled away and the Comet moved forward, Delia saw McArthur, who was occupying the front seat, wave a gloved hand to her.

The engines started to roar as the ferry pilot fed in power and the Comet began to pick up speed on its streamlined wheels. Club members and spectators gave a cheer as the red machine leapt from the grass and with undercarriage retracting, climbed into the late August sky.

Its speed soon became evident as, after making a climbing turn, it dived low across the airfield. Men ducked their heads as it rocketed over them and swept with crackling engines over the neighbouring fields. Delia gave a squeal of pleasure as she turned to Wright. "Isn't she beautiful, Alan?"

Wright glanced at Carlile. "She looks good: I'll say that. But she needs more than looks to beat the pack to Australia. I'll tell you one thing. With that high-wing loading she must be a brute to fly."

Carlile, who had found in the cautious Yorkshireman a kindred spirit, nodded his agreement. "Yeah, that's for sure. I wouldn't like to crash in her either. Not with all that fuel in front of me."

With the aircraft delivered to them at last, Delia could not be subdued. "You're like a couple of old women. She's gorgeous. Just what we need to win the race."

Ten minutes later the Comet swept down and halted at the far end of the field. Through binoculars Delia saw the two pilots jump down to the grass. After talking for a couple of minutes they climbed back in the aircraft. Knowing that McArthur was now taking over, Delia found her nerves tightening as the Comet came taxi-ing towards them.

It halted fifty yards away, then, with a blast of engines, turned to face the wind. A moment later it began rolling forward again.

This time its momentum was not smooth. As its tail-skid rose from the grass, the fuselage began to swing erratically. It ran in this fashion for a couple of hundred yards, then its engine note fell and it came to a halt. Delia glanced anxiously at the two engineers. "What's the trouble?"

"Mac's having problems seeing over her long nose," Carlile told her. "That kid from de Havilland said it makes take-off and landing tricky."

The Comet was swinging round and taxi-ing back for another attempt. Again the tail swung alarmingly from side to side, bringing murmurs from the spectators. Delia found herself whispering to Carlile. "I think he's nervous too. He knows if the plane gets damaged we might be out of the race."

She knew the Texan shared her thoughts. Although the de Havilland company had been working day and night most of that year to have their new aircraft ready in time, only seven weeks were left before the race began. With the company working flat out on remaining orders, a crash of any kind now might mean the end of the couple's ambitions.

It took six attempts before McArthur gathered enough confidence to open up the Comet's engines and lift her from the field. Even so her take-off was hesitant and the plane's thin wings were waggling jerkily as she began climbing. Carlile's anxious growl was made to himself as much as to his companions. "The sonofabitch must be as sensitive as a polecat. Look how he's over-controlling her."

Delia was wondering about the state of McArthur's nerves. During the months since their agreement to fly the race together, he had to her knowledge kept his word and stopped drinking, although what it had cost him in physical and mental terms she could not guess. On the surface, since he and Carlile had arrived in England, his health had seemed to improve but the question she kept asking herself as October drew nearer was how his nerves would stand up when faced with the stress of the race itself.

In many ways it had been an odd year for her. Arriving in England three months before McArthur and Carlile, she had spent them carrying out her lecture tour for the *Daily Mail*. To her surprise she had found Sir Richard Findlay wrong: her public image in Britain had seemed as sharp as ever and huge crowds had greeted her wherever she had travelled.

Heartened by this reception and with little to do regarding the air race until the Comet was delivered, she had allowed a public relations officer to organize other public functions for her in the months ahead. She had found these functions useful on a number of counts. Firstly they paid well and with McArthur and Carlile now in England her expenses were high. She had the Texan's wages to meet and although McArthur might have eliminated his liquor bills, his taste for good living had not diminished. It was true he had offered to share expenses with her but knowing his payments on the Comet were draining him, she had felt obliged to carry the rest of their financial burdens.

The other benefits were considerable. The extra functions had not only kept her image bright in the public eye, they had also given her a legitimate excuse to keep away from McArthur in the waiting period before the Comet arrived. Although it had proved impossible to hide from the press that they slept in different hotel rooms (which had led to immediate speculation of a divorce) the speculation had simmered down when her public programme had provided a legitimate excuse for the two of them being apart.

During this time she had kept in constant touch with Paul, ringing him at least once a week at his office in Philadelphia. With her separation from McArthur keeping her physically as well as mentally lonely, she found this contact a great comfort, although knowing both Carlile and Wright would disapprove, she had mentioned it to neither. One promise she had extracted from Paul brought her great excitement. He intended to be in England when the race to Australia began.

The Comet had now climbed to four thousand feet and was circling the airfield. In her mind's eye Delia was in the cockpit with McArthur, watching him steel himself for the most dangerous part of his test flight, the landing. She doubted that he would be worrying about his personal safety. The Comet represented his last chance to rehabilitate himself and he would be afraid of wrecking that chance by an early accident, as had happened on his Alaskan venture.

Still flying unsteadily, the Comet began to lose height. Its last circuit took it behind the hangar before it levelled off for its landing run. Along with the other spectators and reporters, Delia waited for it to appear. Several seconds passed and then its streamlined shape, with extended wheels and throttled-back engines, came wobbling over the top of the hangar. A grunt from Wright confirmed Delia's own fears. "He's pulling her out too soon."

The Comet, with flaps fully extended, was already in landing position but a good fifteen feet above the grass. Muscles taut, Delia was waiting for the machine to stall or to crumple down on its undercarriage when its engines burst into a startled roar. Hesitating for a moment as if rescue had come too late, the Comet slowly picked up speed and began to climb.

A buzz of comment could be heard from the spectators as the aircraft circled the field again. This time McArthur made no attempt to land. Instead he felt his way by bringing the plane down until her wheels were only feet above the grass and then climbing away again. He repeated this three more times before making another landing attempt. This time he judged his approach better although his wheels thumped the ground so hard that the Comet almost ground looped.

Along with a couple of mechanics, Delia, Carlile and Wright were alongside the plane when its two occupants climbed out. Delia, the first to reach McArthur, saw that his face was shiny with sweat.

He nodded at her question. "Yeah, I couldn't keep her steady. She flies like a goddamned brick."

"Is she going to do the job?" she asked anxiously.

"She's fast enough, that's for sure. And she carries a tanker load of fuel. I guess it all rests whether she lives up to de Havillands' claims."

Bromley was grinning. "She will, sir. I'll lay you a tenner on it."

Delia, itching to fly the plane, glanced at him. "Will you take me up now?"

McArthur broke in before the ferry pilot could answer. "I'd rather you didn't, honey. Bromley can only stay a couple of days so it's better I get used to her first. Besides, we also think she needs a few modifications."

At the time it seemed a reasonable request. "All right," she said. "You get used to her and then you can take me up yourself."

A week passed. The de Havilland pilot had returned to his base but still Delia had not flown in the Comet although by this time McArthur was taking it up several times a day. On the eighth day she became impatient. "All right, I agreed you should learn to fly it first. Don't you think it's my turn now? There's fewer than six weeks to the race."

He prevaricated again. "I'm still not happy with her, baby. Jimmy and Alan think they can still improve her trim. I'd prefer you to wait until they do. I don't want you to have an accident in her."

"What are you worried about? Me or the plane?"

He looked hurt as he stared at her. "Aw, come on, baby.

That's no question to ask."

It was only towards the end of the next week, after she'd had a blazing quarrel with him, that he took her up as a passenger. During the take-off she had to admit the long snout of the aircraft caused problems: until the tail was well off the ground the pilot could see nothing of the runway ahead of him. Airborne, the machine was abnormally sensitive to its controls and it landed at nearly twice the speed of any plane she had flown. If the flight did anything to ease her suspicions, it did nothing to soothe her hurt pride. "All right, she's a racer and she's sensitive. But what makes you think I can't handle her?"

"I didn't say you can't, honey. Only it takes time to get used to a ship like this."

"You've done it in two weeks. Why can't I?"

"Over the years I've flown dozens of different ships. You've only flown Moths and a Bellanca. Both were stable jobs with low landing speeds. This baby comes in like a bullet."

"So what are you saying? That you're not going to let me fly it?"

He turned away restlessly. "Give it a little more time, honey. Let's get her as stable as possible before you take her up."

"You're not going to get her any more stable than she is now. And we haven't any time. The race is barely a month away."

He frowned and turned away. "Don't push things, honey. It's too dangerous."

She had a word with Jimmy Carlile later that day. "He's stalling me, Jimmy. What's his game?"

The Texan showed no doubts. "He's scared you might pile in and kill yourself. That ship's a match winner but it could also be a killer. He doesn't want it to kill you."

"Even if that's true, what makes him think he's a better pilot than I am?" At Carlile's look, she flushed. "I know he's had more experience. But I've plenty of reasons for believing I can fly as well."

"Have you thought of it another way," Carlile asked quietly. "That he's a man trying to take care of his wife?"

She was too angry to give his words any consideration. "I

might have known you'd defend him. I think he's trying to grab all the glory again. Just as he did when we crossed the Atlantic."

Their final quarrel came in the middle of the following week when he allowed her to try her hand after he had taken off and flown the Comet up to eight thousand feet. Knowing how critical he would be, she was in a hypersensitive mood when she took over the dual controls. With the Comet proving even more sensitive than she expected, the result was a slithering about the sky like a high-heeled woman on ice. Nevertheless she believed she was getting the feel of the machine when he tapped her shoulder and indicated she handed control back to him. She shook her head. "No. I must get used to handling her."

"Another day, honey," he shouted. "She's still running away from you."

"The hell she is. You brought her down the first time. So can I."

His bearded face was turning dark with irritation. "Do as I say, for Chrissake."

She pushed the control column forward. "I won't. We're flying this race as partners or have you forgotten?"

Cursing, he grabbed his stick and hauled it back. "Hand over or we'll stay up here all day!"

It was the thought of the sight the Comet would be making to spectators below that finally forced her to obey. White-faced, she said nothing more until he landed and was preparing to taxi towards the hangar. Then she turned on him. "You've planned this all along, haven't you? You've let everyone know you bought the aircraft and now you're letting everyone see you're the pilot who takes it up and lands it. You intend to steal all the glory, just as you did before."

He opened his mouth to protest but her anger was in full cry. "You're stalling off my learning to fly it so that I can't play a full part on October twentieth. But you'll use me once we're airborne, won't you? You accepted my offer to help you and all along you intended to cheat me. Well, it's not going to work. I'm going straight to the press to tell them I'm not flying with you. Our partnership is over, finished."

He gave a violent start. "You can't do that. Not now."

"Can't I? Just wait and see."

"But you'll be cutting your own throat, honey. You'll be out of the race."

All her innate aggression was on the surface now. "Don't you believe it. I know it's your plane and I probably won't get another Comet but there's still time for me to get something else and to register it. And I'm telling the press that's what I'm going to do. I'm going to race against you and if it's the last thing I do, I'm going to beat you."

His cheeks had turned pale. "Then I won't race. Not against you."

"Why?" she sneered. "Because you're afraid I might beat you?" As his features tightened, she went on: "You'd better race or I'll tell the press you're scared of me."

"You bitch," he said.

They were enemies again, using every weapon on hand to hurt one another. "There's another reason you'll race," she said. "You know it's your last chance to get your reputation back. But this time you won't have me to help out when you find you're over the hill. Not this time or ever."

TWENTY FIVE

Delia found Wright in the workshop. "Alan, I've something important to ask you. Will you have dinner with me tonight?"

Wright's eyes were on her face. "Yes, if it's important." He went on without pausing: "You've been crying, haven't you? What's happened?"

She turned away sharply. "I'll tell you over dinner. I'll pick you up at seven-thirty."

She took Wright to a restaurant in Beverley. Although impatient for his decision, she made herself wait until wine was served before coming to the point. "Alan, I'm not flying with Dean in the race. I told him so today."

Wright looked astonished. "You're pulling out? After buying a plane like the Comet? Why?"

"Dean's still in the race. I'm the one pulling out."

"You? But I thought you were so keen to win it."

"I was. But not with Dean. Not now." She went on to explain her change of mind.

Wright looked troubled when she finished. "Are you sure Carlile isn't right? Mac could be worried about your safety."

It was the last thing she wanted to hear from the Yorkshireman. "Don't you start! I know Dean better than any of you. He knows he's gone to the bottom of the ladder and he'll do anything to climb back again."

"If you knew this, why did you make the offer to him in the first place?"

She bit her lip. "I suppose I was feeling sorry for him and thought he had learned his lesson. How wrong can a girl be?"

"But how can you be so sure? That Comet is a brute to fly. The de Havilland pilot said so."

"Alan, he never tried to put the score right when everyone believed he'd just about flown the Atlantic on his own. He took the controls over Nova Scotia when a plane flew alongside us to take photographs. I thought at the time it was just coincidence but now I see it was intentional. And he's doing the same thing again."

When Wright did not speak, her voice rose impatiently. "Why are you looking at me like that?"

"I'm just wondering if you're right in pulling out so near to the race. Won't people feel you're letting him down?"

Her face set. "People will think a damn sight more than that when I've talked to the press. And when they find out I'm going to race against him."

As Wright gave a start, she leaned forward. "That's why I wanted to see you tonight. I want you to be my manager again. Only for a few weeks. To help me get an aircraft that can match the Comet and then fly with me as my co-pilot and engineer."

Wright made an exclamation of protest. "Now wait a minute! I've known things weren't all they should be between you. A blind man can see that. But pulling out and then racing against him! This isn't like you."

"You think it's spiteful, don't you? Maybe it is. But maybe I've got plenty to be spiteful about."

Wright looked both upset and uncomfortable. Certain now he would never agree to her proposition without further evidence against McArthur, she knew she would have to tell him everything although she did not find it easy. "It goes back a long time. Dean has always wanted children but I told him from the beginning I wanted to finish my career first. Then the truth came out about our Atlantic flight; he began drinking heavily; and after the Alaskan fiasco he went right to pieces. It all blew up one night when we had a terrific quarrel." For a moment she hesitated, then her voice hardened. "He demanded that I had a child and when I refused, he raped me."

The conservative in Wright showed in both his shock and embarrassment. "Raped you?"

She stared at him bitterly. "You're like all men, aren't you? You think a wife is there to be used whenever her husband feels like it. It can't be rape if you hold a marriage certificate."

Wright, clearly shaken by this revelation, cleared his throat. "He must want children very badly."

She gave a laugh of disbelief. "Is that all you have to say? He must want children?"

Wright shook his head. "I'm sorry. I didn't mean it the way it sounded."

She lit a cigarette before facing him again. "Now do you see how I feel? If I hadn't forgiven him when we came over, at least I felt I'd given him the chance to get his reputation back. And this is how he rewards me."

Wright's troubled frown deepened. "If only you could be sure he was cheating you."

"I am sure, Alan. As sure as I can be about anything. Now will you help me or must I do it alone?"

"What about my job here? I can't just leave it."

"You can if we tell Sir Richard my plans. He'll know better than anyone the terrific press coverage there'll be when it comes out I'm going to race against my husband. If I promise to advertise one of his products on my aircraft, he'll give you all the leave you want."

He knew she was right. "Then you intend to tell the press everything?"

"Not everything but enough. That we've finally split up and we're entering the race as rivals."

Wright made one last attempt to dissuade her. "Listen to me a minute. The public are tiring of pioneer flights. To thrill them now you've got to take bigger and bigger risks. One of these days you're not going to come back. Why don't you settle down and have children if Mac wants them so much? It would change everything between you."

Her face turned as hard as stone. "No. I don't like being cheated and I intend taking part in this race. Once it's over I intend to divorce him. Then there'll be time to have babies."

His brown eyes seemed to penetrate her mind. "Who with, Delia?"

Her cheeks flushed with guilt. "I don't know. That's something for later. Are you going to help me, Alan, or not?"

The nuggety Yorkshireman sighed. "I never could refuse you anything, could I? Aye, I'll help. But I think you're making a great mistake."

The following morning, after a last effort to see Delia and to change her mind, McArthur flew his Comet down to Hatfield near London, leaving Carlile to sort out the aircraft spares and bring them by truck. Before Carlile left, he had a last word with Delia.

"You're wrong about him this time, kid. He really was worried about your safety."

Liking the Texan, she had no wish to part on bad terms with him. "You must believe what you believe, Jimmy. In any case, he wouldn't do a thing like this to a man. So you're bound to see him in a different light."

"You think that, kid?"

"Yes. He's that kind of man. At heart I don't think he respects women. I can't trust him any more, so it would be stupid to carry on. But I hope we two can stay friends."

"Sure thing, kid. If you enter that race, take care of yourself. It could be tough."

"You too, Jimmy. Good luck to you both."

After a moment's hesitation, the tall Texan leaned down and planted a kiss on her forehead. She squeezed his arm, then watched him climb into his truck and drive away. Her eyes were moist when she turned back to the hangar.

Delia reached forward to the car radio. "Shall we listen to the news?"

Wright, seated beside the girl in her expensive car, shrugged. "Why not?"

She turned the switch. The Greenwich pips sounded the hour, followed by the voice of the newscaster. With the first part of the news bulletin devoted to international affairs, Delia found herself wondering yet again if their journey down to London held any hopes of success.

As she had expected, Sir Richard had given Wright leave of absence for the duration of the race but four precious days had been lost before a stand-in for the engineer had been found. This left only three weeks to find a suitable aircraft, test and modify it, and then to make preparations for the greatest air race in history. At that moment, with rain beating down on the car roof and slanting in the headlights, Delia felt they were on a fool's errand.

The news she was expecting came as she halted the car at a set of traffic lights. "This morning Mrs McArthur, better known as Miss Delia Summers, the record-breaking pilot, startled the aviation world by announcing that she and her husband have separated and no longer intend to fly together on the England-Australia air race scheduled to begin on October twentieth. Instead Miss Summers, as she now wishes to be known, intends to fly her own aircraft in the race. More details of this surprising development are expected in the next two weeks."

The lights changed to green. Switching off the radio, Delia changed gears and the car built up speed again. Beside her Wright's voice was full of reproach. "So you've done it."

Her nod was half hostile, half defensive. "Why not? It would have come out soon enough once I started looking for a plane." When he did not reply, she glanced at him. "Stop being such a conservative old bachelor. Marriages break up every day. Didn't you know?"

Wright's dourness was never more pronounced. "Maybe. But usually for better reasons than yours."

She pretended to misunderstand him. "Dean was cheating me, Alan. I know none of you believe it but he was."

He ignored her evasion. "I wasn't talking about Dean. Have you heard from Paul recently?"

She tried to sound casual. "Yes. I believe he's coming over to England soon."

He stared at her. "You believe?"

Knowing what lay behind his scorn, she suddenly felt malicious. "All right, I know. I had a letter from him two days ago. His holidays are overdue and as he knows I'm taking part in the race, he's decided to come over and see me off. Isn't that nice of him?"

"I suppose you didn't ask him to come?"

"I might have done. I can't remember."

Wright gave a grunt of disgust. "Have you forgotten who you're talking to? Is Gloria coming with him?"

"Not this time. Her father's not well and she feels she ought to stay near him."

A silence fell in which the only sounds were the beating of the rain, the purring of the engine, and the hiss of tyres. Then Wright turned to her again. "I'll tell you something. I don't believe any of this would have happened if you weren't still carrying a torch for Paul. That's why you wouldn't have a baby, wasn't it? Because you were still hoping?"

She gave a start and for a moment her eyes widened. Then she gave a laugh of derision. "Don't talk like a fool. Of course it wasn't."

"I don't believe you. I think you married Mac on the rebound and you've been short changing him ever since. That's why you tear into the poor devil at every opportunity. Because you're ashamed of yourself."

Her anger astonished her. She swung the car into the kerb and halted with a squeal of brakes. "How dare you say things like that? What right have you got?"

As always, Wright did not give an inch. "I've every right. I've known you since you were a skinny kid and I've taught you all you know about engines and aircraft. Sometimes now I wish I hadn't. You'd be a happier girl; I'm certain of it."

She was white to the lips. "Nothing's ever happened between me and Paul. Nothing!"

"Maybe not but I'll lay odds it's not because of you. Can you deny it?"

"Damn you," she shouted. "Get out! Get out of my car!"

Wright threw open the door. As he stepped out into the rain she suddenly reached across and caught his arm. "No. I'm sorry. I didn't mean that."

His face was like carved stone as he stared at her. "Are you sure?"

"Yes. Of course I am. Please, Alan."

Muttering something, he climbed back inside. As she sank down into her seat, she burst into tears. "Stop blaming me, Alan, please. I can't help it. I've tried but I can't."

Realizing her tears were genuine, Wright softened. "I wasn't blaming you. I know these things happen. But it's criminal waste to throw away your life on a happily-married man."

"How do you know he's happily married?" she sobbed.

As much in love with her as ever, Wright wanted to take her

in his arms and comfort her. "There you go again. How do you know he isn't? Why don't you try to accept things as they are? If you don't, you're never going to find any happiness."

The sleeve she drew across her eyes made Wright think of a woebegone child. She sniffed, blew her nose, and then turned to him. "I am happy sometimes, Alan. I'm as happy as a bird when I'm flying."

Wright gave a grunt of disgust. "How long does that last? You need happiness when both your feet are on the ground. And you'll never find it while you're carrying that damned torch."

Impulsively she leaned over and kissed him. "I know you mean well, Alan, and at least you're always honest with me. But stop worrying. Everything's going to be all right after this race."

TWENTY SIX

She phoned Paul from her hotel that evening. "Hello, Paul. No, I'm in London now. Alan's come with me. We're going to look for a plane. I expect you've heard that Dean and I have split up?"

"Yes. The papers here are full of it. What happened?"

"Dean's been up to his old tricks again but it's too long a story to tell now. Are you still coming over?"

"Yes. I dock on the fourteenth. Smudge, isn't it going to be dangerous flying in this race without Mac's experience? Can't the two of you patch it up, at least until the race is over?"

She revelled in his concern. "No. Not this time. I'll be all right if I can find a suitable plane." She paused, then laughed. "I don't suppose you'd be my co-pilot, would you?"

He sounded startled, then laughed back. "Me? Good heavens, no. Not unless you wanted to end up in Iceland."

"We wouldn't. We'd win if you came with me. I know we would."

"Sorry, Smudge. I'm a sober old married man these days. But I'll be there to see you off."

Having had no hope he would accompany her, she was not disappointed. His next words told her Sir Richard had been in touch with him. "As things are, you couldn't go with a better man than Alan, although it's a pity he hasn't Mac's flying experience. What type of aircraft are you looking for?"

"Anything that's fast enough and has enough endurance. The snag is there aren't many of that kind around."

"You know that Father's looking for you as well? He has a lot of contacts so he might come up with something if you've no luck. Personally I hope neither of you has."

She laughed. "Why not?"

"You take too many risks, Smudge. I don't like the sound of this race. I wish you'd give it a miss."

She had one thought when she put the receiver down. Alan

was wrong about Paul. Although he was never one to talk about his feelings, Paul could not have made it clearer that he cared deeply about her welfare and safety. It was a thought she took to bed with her and cradled like a comforting doll before she went to sleep.

A week passed without either her or Wright finding a suitable aircraft. Then, late on Friday afternoon, Sir Richard phoned her. "Well, young lady. What news have you got?"

"I'm afraid we haven't any," she confessed. "We've looked at a few possibilities but none of them would have a chance in the speed race."

"And that's the part you want to win, isn't it?"

"Oh, yes. I'm not interested in the handicap event. I want to be there first."

Sir Richard gave his fruity laugh. "I like that about you, young lady. You don't like second best, do you? Well, I've got good news for you. How would you like another Comet?"

She gave a start. "A Comet! But they're not building any more, are they?"

"They don't need to. One of the chaps who put down a deposit says he doesn't mind losing his if he's given a big enough golden handshake. So I've told my London lawyer to see he gets one. What do you say to that?"

Her eyes were shining like stars. "It's absolutely marvellous. If you were here, Sir Richard, I'd give you the biggest kiss you've ever had. What do we do now?"

"You phone a chap called Stratford at de Havilland. He'll give you the registration number and tell you when they can deliver it to Brook Lane. I'd like you to do your flight trials there so that Wright can keep an eye on the workshop. Don't forget to register it in the race before you come back, will you?"

As if that were likely, she thought. "No, I'll see to everything. What about the cost of the plane, Sir Richard?"

"We'll settle all the details when you get back." Pausing, the tycoon gave a chuckle. "Perhaps when you give me that kiss. Bye-bye now."

She replaced the receiver and hugged herself with joy. The one great obstacle was over. She now had a plane that could match any other in the race, including McArthur's. The rest was up to her and however great the dangers she was determined not to fail.

TWENTY SEVEN

The Comet was circling the airfield at four thousand feet. Two men, Alan Wright and Bromley, were in conversation as they watched it. They were standing apart from club members, reporters, and the public who had congregated at Brook Lane on hearing Delia was beginning her flight trials in her newly-arrived Comet.

The young ferry pilot was showing curiosity. "Why didn't she take you up with her? I thought that was the idea after the instruction I gave her this morning. You are her partner in the race, aren't you?"

In an effort to hide his nervousness, Wright was sucking on his unlit pipe. "She wouldn't risk my skin on her first solo flight. That's the kind of girl she is."

As they watched, the Comet stopped circling and began to descend. Inside the aircraft, Delia was feeling her groin again. She had first felt the pain the previous evening, a faint gnawing ache that had lasted between ten and fifteen minutes. It was sharper now but it disappeared as the airfield rose beneath the long nose of the Comet. She lowered the wheels, changed the airscrew pitch, and steadied herself.

Under his surface calm Wright was as taut as a bowstring as he watched the aircraft come planing down. As its nose tilted up, the young man beside him gave a gasp. "Too early! Give her power!"

As if the girl had heard, the two engines broke into an urgent roar and the Comet went up like a startled bird. Circling the field, it gingerly descended again. This time its wheels touched but the contact was too harsh and again the girl saved an accident only by ramming the throttles forward.

Wright was now in torment as he watched the girl try yet again to land. Again the aircraft's wheels touched but this time it lurched sideways and was saved only by a desperate juggling of engines and controls. Then both wheels were in contact, the tail skid came down and dug into the soft ground, and the Comet came to a shuddering halt.

The young ferry pilot's face was bright with admiration. "She's got guts, that girl. No wonder she got to Cape Town."

Wright could not have replied had he tried. He was spitting out the stem of his pipe which had snapped off between his teeth.

There was great excitement and activity at Mildenhall in Suffolk on the 19th October, the eve of the great race. The excitement was caused by the unexpected arrival of King George V, Queen Mary, and the Prince of Wales. For two hours the frantic efforts to have the entrants and their aircraft ready for take-off at first light the next day had to be suspended while the Royal party moved through the hangars, chatting to the aircrews and inspecting their machines.

The mad activity began again the moment the Royal party drove away. Race officials briefed aircrews and mechanics; AA volunteers arranged aircraft in their order of take-off; crews packed and re-packed their machines with all the complicated equipment demanded by the rules of the competition.

At times, with equipment still lying about on the floors of hangars, it seemed impossible the race could commence on time but, as the day wore on, order began at last to emerge from chaos.

Without an assistant, no one worked harder than Wright. He and Delia had flown into Mildenhall three days ago but Delia had returned to London immediately and only drove back after lunch on the 19th. Her reason was not a dislike of hard work but a wish to avoid contact with McArthur as long as possible.

She was successful until the early evening when he caught sight of her sipping tea in the refreshment tent. Bracing herself, she examined him for signs of drink and general dissipation as he approached her but in a leather flying jacket and corduroy slacks he looked as fit as she had ever seen him. In a way that she did not understand, the sight hardened her heart. "What do you want?" she asked coldly.

He was frowning. "Why wouldn't you talk to me this last couple of weeks? I must have phoned you two dozen times, both at your home and the airfield. And why didn't you answer my letters?''

She shrugged. ''What was there to talk about?''

''Didn't you read my letters? This whole affair's crazy.''

''Since when?'' she asked. ''Since I got an aircraft that can match your own?''

He cursed. ''It's nothing to do with that. It only makes things worse. You can't use Wright as your co-pilot in a Comet. He's only used to toy ships like Tiger Moths.''

''Not any more. He's been testing the Comet with me ever since it arrived.''

''So what? I'll lay odds you've never let him land it?''

''He doesn't need to. All he has to do is spell me in the air. The same as Jimmy will be doing for you.''

''That's different.''

''Why?''

''Because I've got experience of races. And I can last longer.''

''Because you're a man?''

''It helps, yes.''

His sexism brought out the worst in her. ''I didn't notice it helped over the Atlantic.''

His face darkened. ''That's not fair. I was under drugs then.''

''You'll be under drugs this time, if I know you. Don't tell me you haven't a couple of whisky bottles under your seat.''

''That's a lie. I haven't touched a drop since I arrived in England. For God's sake, will you stop throwing punches and listen for a moment?''

She curbed her resentment. ''All right. What do you want?''

''I want to know how equipped you are for this hop. Have you good maps?''

''Of course we have. Do you think we're a couple of fools?''

''What about the emergency airfields? Have you got them all marked? Particularly the ones between Allahabad and Singapore? It's all jungles and mountains out there and we don't know how these new ships are going to measure up.''

Her voice was icy with sarcasm. ''I have done a long-distance flight before, you know.''

''Yeah, but not in a racer like this Comet. This isn't a fourteen-day jaunt. This is go, go all the way.''

''Do you think we don't know it?''

He scowled. "I'm not so sure you do. Wright's a nice guy but he hasn't played this card game before."

"But Jimmy has?"

To her surprise he shook his head. "No, he's new to the game too. That's why I think we're acting crazy. Why don't we bury the hatchet, at least for the next few days, and fly together? I've had a word with the referee and he says it's not too late to make the switch. What do you say? We'd both stand a better chance of winning and it would be a damn sight safer for you."

It was exactly the move she had expected him to make. "And of course it's me you're thinking of?"

"It's a dangerous race, baby. I don't want anything to happen to you."

Her sudden laugh was derisive. "You're quite an operator, aren't you, Dean? For one thing you can't bear the thought of my beating you. But there's more to it than that, isn't there? You can't do it without someone carrying you. Someone good enough but who'll keep his mouth shut afterwards. Someone like me. Isn't that true?"

His brows drew together. "You can't believe that. Not now."

"Wrong. I do believe it. Perhaps if you'd played square with me over the Comet I might have been fool enough to cover you again. But not now. I'm flying with Alan and I'm going to do my best to beat you. That's all. I've nothing more to say."

"God," he said thickly. "What a bitch you've become."

"As I said once before, if I'm a bitch it's what you've made me. Goodbye, Dean."

There was no describing the look he gave her. It seemed to contain anger, fear, and regret in equal proportions. Shaking his head he turned away and made for the tent entrance. Then, fighting back his anger, he hesitated. Turning, he walked back to her.

"What do you want now?" she asked coldly.

He thrust something into her hand. "You'd better have this."

She glanced down. "What is it?"

"A route I've worked out. I reckon it's the quickest and the safest."

"Then why give it to me?"

"Why? It's a trick to get you lost, baby." His bitter voice changed in tone. "At least let Alan see it. He's not a pig-headed fool like you."

She wanted to question him but he was already half-way to the tent entrance. She watched him until his tall figure disappeared into the gloom outside, then gazed down at the map.

The two cigarettes glowed and faded in the dark car. Around it, other cars stretched out into the darkness. On the roads that surrounded the airfield, headlights moved slowly, searching for a vacant space. The air race to Australia was in itself an exciting and unique event. With the McArthurs having declared their intent to compete against one another, it also had a piquant quality that had caught the public imagination. In spite of the inclement weather – it was very cold and overcast for October – many spectators had been in position since the previous day.

Delia was listening to the silence inside the car and the hum of cars and voices outside. In three hours, perhaps less, she would be part of a machine hurling itself through dangerous skies to an unknown fate. The nearness of the adventure seemed to make the tranquillity of the moment the sweeter.

The smell of leather and her feeling of contentment reminded her of another night that she had spent in a car with Paul. It had been many years ago and yet it could have been yesterday for any change in her feelings for him. The emotion of it was in her voice when she broke the silence. "Thank you for coming, Paul. It means so much to me."

His silhouette turned towards her. He sounded half-amused, half-serious. "I couldn't let Smudge go off on another of her exploits without being there to wish her luck, could I?"

A shudder of longing ran through her. "If only you were flying with me. It wouldn't matter then whether I won or lost."

He laughed. "It would on the day, Smudge. Winning's important to you. That's one reason I wish you were flying with Mac. He's got so much experience behind him."

Unseen in the dark, she stiffened. "Not of this kind of race. In any case, he and I are finished. I'm filing for divorce as soon as I get back."

His cigarette glowed before he answered her. "Yet everybody I've spoken to say he's a changed man since he's been over here."

"Everyone doesn't know him. I do."

"That's true. But he does give the impression of being very

much in love with you."

"He's a funny way of showing it," she said.

Headlights flashed into the car for a moment, illuminating his troubled face. The far-off whistle of a train sounded. He waited until the mournful sound died away before glancing back at her. "Do you know how I've always seen you?"

She snuggled against his shoulder. "No. Tell me."

"I've seen you as an adventurous tomboy on the one hand and a rather lonely little girl on the other. How right am I?"

She snuggled closer. "Too right for comfort," she said. "But what's your point?"

"My point? I suppose I'm thinking that a lonely little girl needs a man to share her life with."

She shrugged. "I don't deny it. But it has to be the right man."

"Is there ever a right man, Smudge? Or a right woman for that matter? Can any of us hope to do more than satisfy one part of the other's personality?"

"Which part does Dean satisfy in me?" she asked bitterly.

"The restless part. The adventurous part. The girl who loves flying. Aren't those things a big part of you?"

"Yes, I suppose they are. But Dean doesn't even match up there. He's a cracked vessel these days and he uses people and drink to hide it."

"Don't we all get chips and cracks as we get older? At least no one can take away from him the things he has done. And isn't he showing a lot of courage by staying in this race? Think what the press will do to him if you win."

It was an aspect she had not considered. Then her voice hardened. "It isn't just that he's up to his old tricks again. It's what he did to me in America. How can a woman respect a man who does a thing like that?"

He nodded. "That's the thing you really can't forgive, isn't it?"

She drew on her cigarette. As she exhaled she felt the pain in her groin again. This time it was as sharp as a stitch or a muscle strain. She shifted her position and the pain eased. "Yes," she said. "I think you're right."

In the darkness he had not noticed her discomfort. "Couldn't his desire for a child have had something to do with it? You did say he was drunk at the time."

For a moment her voice was hostile. "You men stick together, don't you? Alan said the same. I don't know his reason and I don't care. Rape isn't just humiliation. It's a man saying to a woman I can do what I like with you because I'm physically stronger. To me that's unforgivable."

He was remembering her long struggle for sexual equality in her career. "Yes, I can see that. But remember not all women are the same. Some like men to be assertive."

"If you're saying Dean thought me one of them, that's even worse. He can't know me at all. I'm me. A person. Someone who can't bear to be taken without my consent."

Again headlights flashed into the car. As his handsome face faded into shadow again, her voice suddenly faltered. "I think that explains my feelings for you, Paul. You've never once tried to take advantage of me. And yet it would have been so easy for you."

As he gave a start and turned towards her, she threw herself into his arms. "Oh God, Paul, the times I've wanted to. The times I've ached for you. You knew how I felt. I told you that night in the tent. So why didn't you take me?"

When he did not speak she tried to reach up and kiss him but the tightness of his arms prevented her. "Why didn't you, Paul? You love me, don't you?"

"Yes," he said quietly. "I love you, Smudge."

His confession, the first he had given her, was like a potent drug exploding in her veins. The joy of it made her burst into tears. "I knew it. No matter what they all said, I knew you loved me. But why have you waited so long, darling? Why have we wasted all these years?"

pressed close to him, she felt him draw in a deep breath and to hold it as if bracing himself. She tried to draw back. "What is it, darling?"

A hand pressed her head back into his shoulder. "I should have told you this years ago, Smudge. But I was always too much of a coward."

After his confession of love, she had no idea what was coming. "What darling? Tell me."

He seemed to be talking to himself rather than to her. "Whenever I tried, I would always see that little girl with shining eyes and a smudged face. And then I would choke up. I couldn't help it."

She laughed at him. "Darling, little girls grow up quickly. I wanted you that night by the river. And that was a long time ago."

He ran a hand down her wet cheek. "You don't understand, do you?"

Outside a loudspeaker blared, giving details of the weather conditions over France. When the echoes died away she tried again to see his face. "Understand what, darling? What are you trying to say?"

She heard the sound of him swallowing before he answered her. "You were a little trusting girl to me, Smudge. A sweet, adoring child that I couldn't bear to hurt. Can you understand that?"

Puzzled, she laughed again. "But that was stupid, wasn't it? It's ages since I was a little girl. How could you have hurt me when ..." Her voice broke off as a cold hand seemed to grip her. "You're frightening me, Paul. You've just said that you love me. Then what do you mean?"

He winced. "I do love you, Smudge. I've always loved you. Now more than ever. But ..."

Understanding came to her in a vivid flash. "But only as a child or a sister? Not the way a man loves a woman?"

His distress was almost palpable. "Is that so little, Smudge? I can't think of anything I wouldn't do for you."

Panting with shock, she pulled away from him. "Anything except to hold me in your arms and love me? Anything except give me the thing I want most in the world?"

"What can I say but that I'm sorry, Smudge? Gloria said a long time ago I should tell you the truth. But I couldn't bear to hurt you."

Bitterness took the place of shock and his mention of Gloria fed it like oil feeds a fire. "You couldn't bear to hurt me? Do you realize what you've done? You've never let a day pass without my dreaming that one day I'd be in your arms. You've stood in the way of every man I've known. You've ruined my life. And all you can say is you're sorry?"

As his dark head bowed, her voice lashed and flailed him. "You've been my idol. I've worshipped you. And you've let me dream all these years about a love that was never there. You couldn't have been more cruel to me."

He looked pale in the shadowy car. "Yes, I can see that. I've been a weak fool.''

As quickly as it had come, her bitterness disappeared. It left a vacuum in her mind that filled with despair and panic. Without thinking, she threw herself back into his arms. "I'm frightened, Paul. I'm terrified! What am I going to do now?"

Her tears were soaking into his jacket. She heard him sigh. "You must do what I should have let you do years ago. Forget me and give your love elsewhere."

With her emotions swinging like a pendulum, her bitterness returned. "And go through all this again? What kind of a fool do you think I am? I've had my lesson. I don't need another."

Outside the horizon was lightening, silhouetting the line of waiting aircraft. Before either could find anything more to say, the loudspeakers blared out again with instructions that all competitors had to report to the starter's tent.

She felt both relief and despair. "I'll have to go now. Alan will be waiting for me."

His glance was full of unspoken regrets. She checked him before he could speak. "No, don't say any more, Paul. I suppose I'm as much to blame as you for being such a fool. Just wish me luck and leave it there."

Before he could reply, she jumped from the car and began running towards the line of aircraft. A stab of pain in her side forced her to slow down but her mind was suddenly cold and determined. In the past she had given her love too trustingly and it had been abused. Such happiness that life had given her had come mainly from flying, not from men.

From now on that would all change. She would use men but now only to prove she was their equal. And what better opportunity for that than the race ahead? Determined as never before, she went in search of Alan Wright.

TWENTY EIGHT

From above, the wooded hills of Assam looked like a crumpled velvet carpet. Wright leaned forward. "She's going like a sewing machine. If she keeps this up I think we've got a chance."

Delia pulled herself together. There was something almost reassuring in the Yorkshireman's caution. "What do you mean – a chance? We're going to win."

"Don't get too confident," Wright warned. "We've still a long way to go."

At that moment she had never felt less confident but was determined to keep the reason from Wright as long as possible. "We're in the lead, aren't we? Why shouldn't we win?"

In fact they had been in the lead since they left Mildenhall, for Delia had been drawn first for take-off. Concerned that the other competitors might believe she had been favoured because of her sex, she had sought out the referee, only to be assured that the draw had been made without fear or favour. She had also been reminded that the few minutes gained at the take-off would be struck off when the speed winner was decided: in other words the lead was only illusory.

Accordingly she had flown *Hermes*, the name she had bestowed on her Comet, out of Mildenhall at 05.30 to the wild acclaim of sixty thousand spectators who were now crowded on and around the airfield. Knowing McArthur and the other Comet crews, as well as the Boeing and Douglas airliners, would be in hot pursuit, they had not spared *Hermes* in the race for the first compulsory control point, Baghdad, but to their relief the Comet had behaved impeccably, a tribute, she felt, not only to its designer and manufacturer but also to Wright who had spent many dedicated hours checking and tuning its engines.

Until they reached Allahabad, the second control point, they had not used McArthur's route. With her wish to prove herself on every count, Delia had not wanted to use it at all but here Wright's common sense had prevailed. "I've checked it and it looks good to me. If we ignore it, we'll be handicapping ourselves. Where's the sense in that?"

The map had proved unnecessary over Europe and the Middle East. In such a populated area as Europe, there had been more than enough landmarks to help them. Even over the Middle East, where deserts were largely unmapped and contained few landmarks, they had found few difficulties. The RAF had run cars and in some cases tractors across the oceans of sand to leave tracks visible from the air. Inevitably here and there the tracks had been obliterated by sandstorms but by flying low and with the help of Wright, who proved to have excellent night vision, she had always managed to find them again.

As a result they had reached Baghdad in twelve and a half hours, nearly an hour ahead of McArthur who was leading the pack behind them. With such intense competition there was no time to rest. Delia had taken a quick bath, then joined Wright in a meal of sandwiches and coffee while *Hermes* was being refuelled. Ninety minutes after their arrival they were in the air again. With the Comet having proved the endurance her three fuel tanks provided, they had decided to omit the refuelling stops and make straight for Allahabad.

On this leg Delia had allowed Wright to take over the controls once they had reached a safe altitude. He did not handle the aircraft with her confidence but he had mastered it sufficiently to keep it flying a straight course while she took a rest, although rest was a relative word. With Wright needing to concentrate on flying the difficult Comet, she was afraid he might stray off course and so had made herself stay awake to keep an eye on his navigation.

As yet staying awake had not proved a problem. The twinges of pain in her groin, which earlier had been only spasmodic, had now settled into a persistent ache. It had spread across her lower abdomen and become particularly painful when she used her right leg. Although still bearable, she had no longer been able to deceive herself that it was merely a strain and could only pray it did not grow worse before she reached Australia.

On landing at Allahabad, they had learned that McArthur was now a mere thirty minutes behind them. When Wright had broken the news, her reply had been rueful. "It looks as if I was wrong about one thing. He seems to be managing well enough without me."

Wright had not disagreed. "I've thought all along that you were underestimating him. You can't deny the man's record. Now he's laid off the drink he could be his old self again."

With pain nagging her, there had been a feverish quality to her determination. "I'm not going to let him beat me, Alan." She had nodded at the mechanics clustered around *Hermes*. "Tell them to hurry up, please. We can't afford to waste a minute."

The dramatic change in her condition had come as she was making for the refreshment hall. Not seeing a picketing hook, she had stumbled over it and immediately a shock of pain had doubled her up. Painkillers had helped her climb up into the forward seat but only with difficulty, and she had been certain Wright would have noticed her pain had he not been talking to the RAF Met. officer at the time. She had climbed as quickly as possible to four thousand feet and then, using fatigue as her excuse, had asked Wright to take over. Now, four hours out of Allahabad, the severity of the pain was making her fumble into the pocket of her overalls for more drugs.

Seated behind her, Wright watched her surreptitiously put tablets into her mouth and then wash them down with a cup of coffee. Unknown to her, he had noticed her discomfort when climbing into the cockpit but Wright, a bachelor, had made the assumption her problem was a feminine one. He knew some women had periods more troublesome than others and for all he knew Delia might be one of them.

Consequently he had not been too concerned. He knew the girl's courage and although it would be embarrassing for her, he had little fear that such a natural occurrence would prevent her from completing the race.

Now he was not so sure. When not flying herself, Delia had shown her eagerness to win by checking every landmark along their route. Now she was doubled forward, with her knees drawn up almost to her chin. Reaching forward he touched her shoulder. "Delia. Are you all right?"

At first she did not move. Alarmed now, Wright shook her. "Delia! What's the trouble?"

This time she stirred. Her lips moved but the engines drowned her words.

Wright stared at the pale, sweating face half-turned towards him. "For God's sake, what is it, girl?"

In the speaking tube her voice was weak and halting. "I don't know, Alan. I've got a pain in my side. It seems to have got much worse since Allahabad."

"When did it start?"

"A few days ago. But it wasn't bad then."

"Why didn't you tell me?"

She tried to smile. Wright swore. "That was daft. What's a bloody race against your health? Have you had anything like it before?"

To his alarm she shook her head. Taking another look at her, Wright grabbed his map. She gave a start. "What are you doing?"

"You need a doctor to look at you. There should be one at the next emergency airfield."

She protested immediately. "No. We're in the lead. You mustn't lose it."

"Damn that. I'm going to get you to a doctor."

"No, Alan, please. At least wait until we get to Singapore. I'll see a doctor there if it gets any worse. Don't spoil things now. Please, Alan."

With his love for her tugging at him from both sides, Wright hesitated. At that moment, and with his attention distracted, the Comet took its chance and lurched violently to port. The jerk, throwing the girl against her safety straps, brought a cry of agony from her. White-faced, certain now what he must do, Wright regained control, then glanced at McArthur's map again. "We're going down at the next emergency field. We should reach it in about twenty minutes."

She fought him feverishly. "No, Alan. Please." When he

ignored her, her voice rose. "It's my aircraft, damn you, and I'm in charge. I'm ordering you to go on to Singapore."

Wright shook his head and advanced the throttles. Ignoring her pain, she caught hold of the dual control. For a few seconds the Comet slithered all over the sky. Then, finding his strength was too much for her, she released the column. As the Comet steadied, she gave a feverish laugh. "You've forgotten: you can't land her. And I won't land until we reach Singapore."

Wright was sweating with tension. "I'll land her. Somehow."

"You can't land a Comet. You'll kill us both if you try."

Eyeing her drawn, pain-racked face, Wright was beginning to think she would die if he didn't. "I'll get us down," he said grimly. "One way or the other."

TWENTY NINE

Wright caught sight of the emergency landing-strip eighteen minutes later. From their height and distance it looked like a brown strip of ribbon lying on a bottle-green quilt but as the Comet ate up the miles it turned out to be a dusty cutting in the dense trees. Two buildings and a tent stood along its north side. The larger building had a wind sock flying above it. The second had a large red cross painted on its roof. As Wright circled the strip he hoped fervently that there was a crash wagon and an ambulance on stand-by.

His comment and manoeuvre revived Delia from her pain and she struggled upright to see the landing strip. As Wright banked to give her a view, she gave a laugh of derision. "You don't think you can set her down on that, do you?"

Wright levelled the Comet and turned to her. "One of us is going to. I'd rather it was you. If I let you take over, will you promise me there'll be no funny business and you'll land her?"

Without answering his question, she took hold of the control column again. Frowning, Wright repeated his question. "Do you promise?"

Pain made her cry aloud. "For God's sake stop arguing and let me take over."

To reach the rudder controls she had to straighten her body and lift her legs. As she made the effort, trying to lever her right leg up with her hand, she gave a cry of agony and doubled up again. It was more than enough for Wright. "That's it then. I have to land her. Sit there quiet and guide me down."

Although feeble with pain now, she still tried to fight him. "You'll kill us both. Fly on to Singapore. It's a bigger field there."

Tension snapped Wright's self-control. "Shut up about Singapore. I've had a bellyful of you and McArthur acting like a couple of daft kids trying to prove who's top dog. Who cares who wins the bloody race? Who'll even remember in two years time?"

In her pain and astonishment at his outburst, she looked almost childlike as she stared back at him. Wright's voice softened. "Don't you realize you've probably got appendicitis? If it bursts, if it hasn't already, every minute's important because you're going to need urgent surgery. So stop arguing and help me land this thing. All right?"

He saw her give a sullen nod of consent. Not daring to think what he was doing, Wright glanced down at the wind sock, drew back the throttles, and pushed the column forward.

His first attempt to land was a total failure. Afraid of catching the trees at the approach end of the strip, he levelled off too late, giving the fast Comet too little runway for a touchdown.

His second attempt was equally abortive. By this time a dozen men had run out of the buildings and were staring up and gesticulating. A brown truck and an ambulance had also emerged from the smaller building and were now parking at the far end of the airstrip, a grim hint of what their crews expected.

On Wright's third attempt he managed to touch the dirt with his wheels but the high landing speed of the Comet forced him to jerk her back into the air to avoid the on-rushing trees.

By this time Wright was sweating as freely as the pain-racked girl in front of him. It was apparent that the landing strip, no doubt hacked from the forest at great expense, had been restricted to the absolute minimum length commensurate with safety. With the Comet's thin wings giving it such a high landing speed, only a highly-skilled pilot accustomed to the aircraft was likely to land it without accident.

Realizing it, Wright made his decision. "I'm going to crash-land," he told the girl. "So tighten your straps. If it works out as I hope, it shouldn't be too bad."

Her eyes, swimming with pain, gazed back at him

questioningly. Wright pointed at the two engines. "You see they're underslung. That means if I draw up the wheels, they should strike the ground first instead of the fuselage. If my guess is right, the wings will then take the shock. If they hold, we'll get off lightly. Even if they don't, they should cushion the impact. Shall we try it?"

Her sweat-soaked head nodded. Wright tried to show confidence he did not feel. "It'll work. I'm sure of it. Are your straps tight?"

She nodded again and even managed a smile. With a lump in his throat, Wright reached forward and ruffled her wet hair. Then he tightened his own straps. "All right. Here we go."

To get his nerves under control, he took the Comet on a wide circuit. He retracted the wheels into their nacelles and vented his fuel tanks. Then, giving Delia a reassuring smile, he headed back for the landing strip.

He saw men waving frantically as he came in low over the trees and knew they were trying to warn him that his wheels were retracted. Deciding that this time he would take advantage of every foot of the runway, he lowered the Comet until he became afraid its spinning propellers might catch the upper branches of the trees. From the corner of his eye he saw the rigid figure of Delia and knew that whatever the state of his nerves, she, as the passenger, would be suffering the most.

The last of the trees slid beneath him and the dusty strip unfolded like a giant roller coaster. Gritting his teeth he kept the column forward until the last moment: with the tanks vented of petrol it was unlikely the engines would take him round a second time. He switched off both of them and waited until he could see tiny stones on the dirt runway. Then he heaved back on the column.

The Comet's long nose rose and for a moment she seemed to hang in the air. Then, to a sinking feeling in the stomach, she dropped like a stone.

A second later everything seemed to happen at once. There was a massive thud as the two engines dug into the earth, a violent jolting and rocking, the snapping of spars, and a cloud of brown dust that blanketed the canopy. Through it all, as if Wright's senses had been listening for nothing else, there was a cry of agony from Delia. Although flung about himself in the cockpit, Wright tried desperately to reach forward and prevent the girl from further pain as the Comet did a final dizzy ground loop before coming to a halt.

Snapping open the buckle of his straps, Wright leaned over the slumped girl. "Delia! Are you all right?"

To his distress he saw her eyes were closed. "Delia! Can you hear me?"

Outside there was the squeal of brakes as the ambulance and crash wagon arrived. At the same moment Delia's eyes opened. To Wright's disbelief she managed a smile. "Well done, Alan. That was a terrific landing."

For once all Wright's northern reserve deserted him as he hugged her. "You're the tops, lass. The bravest girl I've ever known." Then he threw back the canopy and shouted through the cloud of choking dust. "Get this girl out and into the ambulance. As fast as you can!"

Wright took an anxious step forward as the English doctor jumped down from the ambulance. "How is she, Doctor?"

The man, small, thin-faced, wearing a white linen suit and topee, was clearly resenting his temporary residence on the hot, fly-ridden airstrip. "How long has she been in this condition?"

"I think she said the pain started a few days ago."

Wright received and irritable stare. "Then what on earth is she doing in this race?"

Wright was in no mood for an interrogation. "What's wrong with her? Is it appendicitis?"

"Of course it is. It's a disgrace she was ever allowed to fly. Why didn't she report her symptoms to the race authorities?"

Wright's effort to control his temper was medal-worthy. "Does she need an operation?"

"Good God, man, of course she does. She also needs proper hospital facilities. And they're sixty miles away across dirt roads. Do you realize what that means?"

Wright went very pale. "She'll survive it, won't she?"

The man's thin shoulders lifted. "How can I say that? I've given her an injection to ease the pain but that's not the problem. Do you realize how bad roads can be out here?"

By this time sweat was trickling down Wright's forehead. "Then shouldn't we be on our way?"

The man gave another irascible frown. "We'll go as soon as I've sent off my wireless report. Don't forget there could be equally irresponsible competitors dropping in here before the day's out."

To clear the runway in case such an event happened, the airstrip's ground crew were attaching towing ropes to the crashed Comet so that a tractor could drag it aside. As the doctor made towards the main building, Wright entered the ambulance. He expected to find Delia asleep after her injection but her eyes opened as he sank down beside her. "How are you feeling now?"

Her voice was very weak. "Not too bad. But I've got appendicitis and have to go to hospital. Has the doctor told you?"

Wright nodded. "We're leaving as soon as he's sent off his report."

She sounded wistful. "Then you are coming with me?"

"No," he said. "I'm going to sit in *Hermes* and do a crossword puzzle."

She tried to smile, then her voice broke. "I'm sorry, Alan."

"What for? For being taken ill?"

"No. I'm just sorry for everything. It's all fallen apart, hasn't it?"

"Not for me it hasn't. I couldn't care less about the race."

"But it would have been nice for us to win, wouldn't it? And we were leading. Now Dean's sure to get there first."

He was watching her wan face, stripped by pain of all bitterness and acrimony. "Wouldn't you rather he won than anyone else now?"

She gave a wince of pain, then nodded her head wearily. "Yes, I think so. It would be better than nothing, wouldn't it?" Then she noticed Wright listening. "What is it?"

Wright went to the rear door. The sound of aero engines were growing louder. A moment later a Comet appeared, swooping low over the airstrip before going into a climbing turn. As Wright glanced at his watch, there was a weak cry from Delia. "Is it Dean, Alan?"

Wright was trying to read the aircraft's identification letters. "Yes, it must be. He was due about now."

The girl struggled to rise. "Help me up, please."

Afraid to move her, Wright hesitated and then realized she might do herself more harm if he did not. He eased her up gently until she could see from the side window. Her confused expression told him that pain and drugs were taking their effect. "What's he doing, Alan? He isn't out of fuel, is he?"

Having completed its surveillance of the airstrip, the Comet was coming in to land but not in the usual fashion. It was side-slipping over the flanking trees with blipping engines giving it control. At the last moment it straightened out, its engines blipped a last time, and in a long plume of dust it settled down to a perfect three-point landing.

Delia's feverish eyes turned on Wright. "I don't understand, Alan. Why has he landed?"

Wright eased her back on her pillow. "Isn't it obvious? He's seen we've crashed and he wants to find out how you are. Lie still and I'll go and fetch him."

Outside McArthur had not wasted a moment. Swinging the Comet round, he was taxi-ing at speed towards the parked ambulance. As Wright ran alongside the plane, the American leapt to the ground. "Where's Delia? Is she hurt?"

Wright explained as briefly as he could. Before he finished McArthur began running towards the ambulance. The concerned voice of Carlile at his elbow made Wright turn. "What's the score, Alan? Is she going to be O.K.?"

"God knows," Wright said. "She needs surgery badly and soon."

The Texan winced. "If you hadn't used Mac's route we'd never have known about it."

McArthur reached the ambulance at the same time as the doctor who had made his wireless report. Both men disappeared into the vehicle, to emerge half a minute later. As they moved a few paces away, their expressions and gestures made it clear they were having a fierce argument. It ended with McArthur pushing the doctor away, jumping into the ambulance, and driving it at speed towards his aircraft. Halting it a few yards away, he leapt out and shouted at Wright and Carlile. "Give me a hand with Delia! I want her lifting into my ship. As gently as you can."

Wright caught his arm. "Where are you taking her? Singapore's too far. And Allahabad's nearly five hours away."

McArthur threw off his arm. "She's going to the hospital. I can get her there in twenty minutes."

"But can you get off this field? And where will you land?"

Irascible in his concern for the girl, the bearded American cursed. "Stop asking goddamn questions. The MO says there's a race course near the hospital. I'll put her down there."

By this time the ground crew had abandoned the crashed *Hermes* and were congregating round McArthur's Comet. With their help the barely conscious Delia was lifted into the cockpit. Before McArthur could climb in after her, Wright made sure he was the one to fasten her safety straps. "Are you going to be all right?" he muttered.

Her dazed eyes told him she was delirious. "What's happening, Alan? Why am I flying with Dean again?"

Wright had no chance to answer. Pushing him aside, McArthur swung up into the cockpit. Seconds later he started the engines and began taxi-ing back along the airstrip. Carlile, who had been giving instructions to the crew, caught Wright's arm. "He needs our help, Alan. Let's go."

Puzzled, Wright followed the men running after the Comet. As the aircraft swung round at the extreme end of the dirt strip and men grabbed its tail unit, he understood. To gain flying speed as soon as possible, McArthur was going to open up his engines while the Comet was still standing in the chocks. The ground crew's job was to hold the tail down from lifting in the slipstream and turning the aircraft over.

The roar of the engines grew louder. Dust came funnelling back, choking the men's eyes and nostrils. Alongside the wheels, Carlile and a mechanic were crouched down, holding the ropes that led to the chocks. At a signal from McArthur, they both jerked the chocks away and the Comet leapt forward like a sprinter from his blocks.

Shielding his grit-filled eyes, Wright watched the plane gathering speed. With a long plume of dust dragging behind it, it was difficult to judge its speed and for one horrific moment Wright believed it was going to crash into the far trees. Then, quite suddenly, the plume of dust swept upwards in a graceful curve and the Comet emerged from it intact in the bright sky.

Wright and Carlile exchanged glances. The Texan's obscenity was an effort to hide his emotion. "Goddamn it, did you see that? And the landing he made? The sonofabitch has got it all together again."

Wright's reaction was equally basic. "I need a drink." He nodded at the administration building. "I wonder if they stock whisky over there. Let's go and find out."

THIRTY

Encouraged by the smiling Indian nurse, McArthur opened the door of Delia's private ward and stepped inside. Thinking she was asleep he tiptoed forward, only to halt when she turned her head towards him. "Hello, Dean." Then, seeing his concern: "It's all right. I wasn't asleep."

He moved to her bedside, bent down, and kissed her. Looking slightly self-conscious, he indicated the spray of roses he was carrying. "What shall I do with these?"

She took them from him. "Thank you. They're beautiful." She laid them on the cabinet. "The nurse will put them in water later on."

He sank into a chair. "I thought they were never going to let me see you."

"Yes. It's four days, isn't it?"

"Yeah. You had a rough passage, honey. Wright and me have been worried sick about you."

They were as shy as strangers talking to one another, she thought. "Where is Alan?"

"In the waiting-room. He's hoping to see you afterwards."

She gave a wan smile. "Has he told you how I argued with him to keep on going?"

"He didn't need to, honey. I've seen you in action before."

"It's a good thing he took no notice. The surgeon said if we'd gone on I wouldn't be alive today."

"Yeah. He told me the same."

"He told me something else too," she said. "That if I'd been forced to come by ambulance, the journey would have killed me."

He avoided her eyes. "Yeah, they say the roads are bad."

There was a pause, then she said quietly: "I'm sorry, Dean."

"Sorry, honey? What for?"

"I know what the race meant to you. You must feel awful losing it this way."

He raised an eyebrow. "Lose it, honey? I thought we'd won it."

Still weak from her illness, she felt her eyes burning. "That's a lovely way to put it, Dean. But I still feel dreadful for you."

He grinned. "You do, honey? I thought you were the girl who was trying to beat me."

With the things she had to say to him, she was grateful he was treating the occasion in a light-hearted way. In her present state she doubted if she could have faced a more sober meeting.

"I was," she said. "And I would have done if this damned appendix hadn't spoilt everything."

His laugh reminded her how she had always liked his sense of humour. "So why are you sorry now?"

"There are ways and ways of beating you. I'd be a bit of a heel if I was glad it happened this way, wouldn't I?"

"You've a point there, kid. Yeah, I think you would."

Her tone changed. "It's your sponsors I'm worried about. They must feel you've cheated them. After all, you were leading the field after I dropped out."

He grinned again. "You've still a lot to learn. I don't suppose you've seen any English newspapers since your operation?"

"No. What are they saying?"

"They're purring, honey. Like a fat cat with a bowl of cream."

"Purring? I don't understand."

"Don't you see, kid, the press and the sponsors have never had it so good. My hotel phone's never stopped ringing these last few days. We've given 'em an entire screen scenario."

Suddenly she understood. First they had given the world success and romance. Then quarrels and separation. Now, to cap everything, a dramatic crash and an even more dramatic sacrifice.

In her weakened state, the entire affair suddenly seemed ludicrous and a giggle broke from her. "So that was why you came down to help me?"

"You catch on quick, honey. Did you think I'd gone sentimental on you?"

She giggled again, then winced as her stitches hurt. Noticing it, his tone changed. "You all right, baby?"

His concern made her eyes burn again. Angry with herself, she fumbled beneath her pillow for a handkerchief. Unable to find it, she accepted the one he offered her and blew her nose hard. "Yes, of course I am. How is Alan?"

"He's fine. Like me, he's been worried about you but he's on top of the world now."

She knew she must say it soon but it was proving harder than she thought. She took a deep breath. "I've done a lot of soul-searching these last two days, Dean. And I've realized I haven't always played fair with you."

He looked almost embarrassed by her confession. "Aw, come on, honey. It's me that's given you a hard time."

"Yes but I can see now how much of that was my fault. For one thing I don't think I let you know before we married just how strong my ambitions were."

"You're kidding, honey. You flew the big fish pond with me. Remember?"

"All right, but I never told you what an independent person I am. Did I?"

He hesitated, then gave a wry shrug. "Shouldn't I have seen that myself?"

"No, how could you? It was something you never expected in a woman." She paused, then met his eyes squarely. "The thing is, Dean, I can't change. If I promised otherwise, I'd be a liar."

His expression defied analysis. "Is this what you wanted to tell me?"

She blew her nose again. "Yes. I suppose I wanted to ease my conscience."

He grinned. "How does it feel now?"

"What?"

"Your conscience."

She stared at him indignantly. "I notice you've done nothing to ease yours."

He took her hand. "It would take me the rest of the day to admit my faults, honey. Do you want me to start?"

She did not draw her hand away. "No, don't bother. In any case I know them."

His eyes were searching her face. Behind them was a desire he could not hide. "Yeah, I guess you do. I've given you a rough ride, baby. But you were right. I'd never met a girl like you before."

Sure of him now, she decided womanlike to play him a little longer. "It was too much for you, wasn't it, Dean?"

"I wouldn't say that, honey. It just took some getting used to, that's all. But I was working on it at the end."

"Did you make it?"

"Yeah, I think so. Like giving a loose rein and that kind of thing."

"No," she said sharply. "No reins. Not for either of us." Then, seeing his expression, her tone changed. "I know it must be hell for a macho character like you but there's no other way for me."

He grinned ruefully. "O.K., honey. No reins."

She decided she had held him in suspense long enough. "Do you know what Paul said to me?"

"Paul?"

"Yes. We had a long talk before the race. He said you were right for me because you appealed to the side of me that liked change and adventure."

He gave a start. "Paul said that? The guy's smarter than I thought."

"He said a lot more too." For the first time she realized she could face it without pain. "He told me that for all these years he'd never seen me as anything but a kid sister."

He winced. "That must have hurt, baby."

"It did but it also made me grow up and see the mistakes I've made. If I wanted certain rights in marriage, I had to allow you rights too. There has to be some give and take."

"I'm not sure I'd want my rights again, honey. They haven't done me much good so far."

She gripped his hand. "There's one right I think you'd want. If we did decide to try again, that is."

His voice was suddenly eager. "What's that?"

"That baby you've been fretting about for so long. This time I wouldn't be so selfish. I'd have it first and then we could sit down and work the rest out."

She had never seen his face so eager and heartfelt. "Are you serious, honey?"

"Yes, of course I am. So what do you want to do? Shall we give it another try?"

His answer was a laugh loud enough to be heard all over the hospital. Leaning forward, he grabbed her and planted his mouth on her lips. For a moment she responded as passionately but then found she could not breathe. Struggling, she managed at last to free herself and to push him away. "Have you gone crazy?" she gasped. "I didn't mean here and now. At least wait until they've taken my stitches out!"

Their laughter could be heard in the waiting-room where Wright was seated. Rising, he walked out into the corridor where he heard a fresh peal of laughter. For a moment he felt a twinge of envy, then it was gone. An old bachelor like himself, set and comfortable in his ways, could never have given her happiness. She would have been like a bird in a cage and sooner or later would have grown to hate the bars that were imprisoning her. Whereas love kept only in the mind was always free to explore the woods and scale the mountains.

He glanced at his watch. Visiting time was almost over. He would not steal any of it from them: instead he would come back tomorrow when she was stronger.

Turning, he walked down the corridor and out into the grounds where the hot sunlight was bringing out the incense of hibiscus and frangipani. Wright glanced around him and breathed deeply. She was well again and she was happy. It was good to be alive.